"If you insist   **it's going to be me!"**

"No—" Lizzie tried to say, but Joe kissed her again until she was a pool of frustrated desire.

"If you keep up your charade, I'm going to have to go back down there and tell them all what's going on." He cupped her face with one hand. "Is that what you want?"

Lizzie knew what she wanted, and it had nothing to do with truth telling. It had to do with ripping off Joe's clothes and kissing him from stem to stern. She let her gaze trail over him. Oh, he was good-looking and very sexy. No question about that. He took her breath away.

But when she looked at Joe, she also saw trust and affection and something she could really hold on to. Refuge.

In a world gone mad, Joe was the sanest thing going.

"Joe," she asked hopefully, "can I stay with you tonight?"

Lizzie hadn't planned for anything more than that to happen, but there was a gorgeous breeze blowing the curtains at his cottage, a full moon peeking through the trees, milk and chocolate chip cookies…and a really fabulous brass bed.

Before she knew it, Lizzie was seducing Joe, as if she was his real bride-to-be.

Dear Reader,

Weddings in any family are a celebration, but in the Bellamy family, be prepared for surprises. The Bellamys have been known to be outrageous! And this wedding's no exception—complete with a bachelor, a baby and a bodyguard!

Join in the fun with THE WEDDING PARTY, a new trilogy by three of your favorite American Romance authors. Julie Kistler, Pamela Browning and Jacqueline Diamond will take you through all the weekend festivities.

Julie Kistler leads off the trilogy. Julie loves combining comedy with fantasy to create her own unique style. She's been writing for American Romance for ten years. Along with her husband, she lives in Illinois.

Be sure to catch the upcoming titles in THE WEDDING PARTY: *RSVP...Baby* by Pamela Browning and *Assignment: Groom!* by Jacqueline Diamond.

Sincerely,

Debra Matteucci
Senior Editor & Editorial Coordinator
Harlequin Books
300 East 42nd Street
New York, NY 10017

Last-Chance
Lizzie's Fiancé

JULIE KISTLER

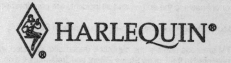

HARLEQUIN®

TORONTO • NEW YORK • LONDON
AMSTERDAM • PARIS • SYDNEY • HAMBURG
STOCKHOLM • ATHENS • TOKYO • MILAN • MADRID
PRAGUE • WARSAW • BUDAPEST • AUCKLAND

If you purchased this book without a cover you should be aware
that this book is stolen property. It was reported as "unsold and
destroyed" to the publisher, and neither the author nor the
publisher has received any payment for this "stripped book."

ISBN 0-373-16782-2

LIZZIE'S LAST-CHANCE FIANCÉ

Copyright © 1999 by Julie Kistler

All rights reserved. Except for use in any review, the reproduction or
utilization of this work in whole or in part in any form by any electronic,
mechanical or other means, now known or hereafter invented, including
xerography, photocopying and recording, or in any information storage
or retrieval system, is forbidden without the written permission of the
publisher, Harlequin Enterprises Limited, 225 Duncan Mill Road,
Don Mills, Ontario, Canada M3B 3K9.

All characters in this book have no existence outside the imagination of
the author and have no relation whatsoever to anyone bearing the same
name or names. They are not even distantly inspired by any individual
known or unknown to the author, and all incidents are pure invention.

This edition published by arrangement with Harlequin Books S.A.

® and TM are trademarks of the publisher. Trademarks indicated with
® are registered in the United States Patent and Trademark Office, the
Canadian Trade Marks Office and in other countries.

Look us up on-line at: http://www.romance.net

Printed in U.S.A.

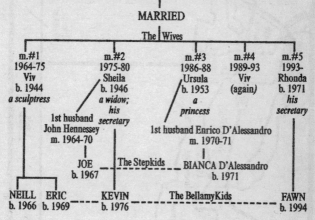

WILLIAM "BUDGE" BELLAMY aka The Pretzel King b. 1939

MARRIED

The Wives

| m.#1 1964-75 Viv b. 1944 a sculptress | m.#2 1975-80 Sheila b. 1946 a widow; his secretary | m.#3 1986-88 Ursula b. 1953 a princess | m.#4 1989-93 Viv (again) | m.#5 1993- Rhonda b. 1971 his secretary |

1st husband John Hennessey m. 1964-70

1st husband Enrico D'Alessandro m. 1970-71

JOE b. 1967 — The Stepkids — BIANCA D'Alessandro b. 1971

NEILL b. 1966   ERIC b. 1969   KEVIN b. 1976   The BellamyKids   FAWN b. 1994

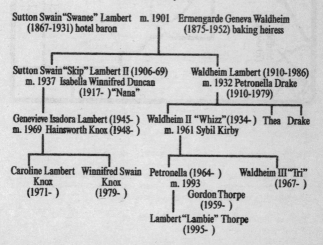

Lambert Family Tree

Sutton Swain "Swanee" Lambert (1867-1931) hotel baron   m. 1901   Ermengarde Geneva Waldheim (1875-1952) baking heiress

Sutton Swain "Skip" Lambert II (1906-69) m. 1937 Isabella Winnifred Duncan (1917-) "Nana"

Waldheim Lambert (1910-1986) m. 1932 Petronella Drake (1910-1979)

Genevieve Isadora Lambert (1945-) m. 1969 Hainsworth Knox (1948-)

Waldheim II "Whizz" (1934-) m. 1961 Sybil Kirby

Thea Drake

Caroline Lambert Knox (1971-)   Winnifred Swain Knox (1979-)   Petronella (1964-) m. 1993 Gordon Thorpe (1959-)   Waldheim III "Tri" (1967-)

Lambert "Lambie" Thorpe (1995-)

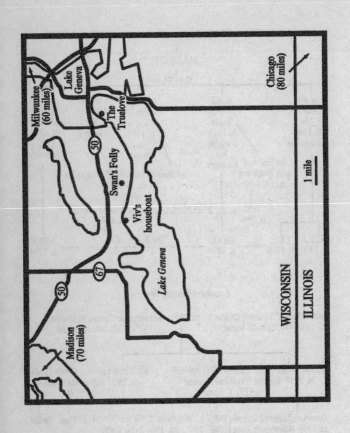

Chapter One

Prewedding jitters

There were messages piled up on her desk, her phone had been ringing all morning, and she had meetings scheduled out the wazoo.

But for once in her life, Elizabeth Rose Muldoon was determined to ignore every single call for help. For once in her life, she was going to concentrate on her own problems.

Stuck between a rock and a hard place. Rock: she had agreed to be a bridesmaid in the wedding of the millennium. Hard place: she had a major crush on the groom.

What could she do?

"Lizzie?" The intercom buzzed again, and she heard her secretary's harried, squeaky voice. "I've got Dick from Accounting on line one. Please pick up!"

Dick was one of Lizzie's pet projects, one of those folks she'd hired when no one else would. Okay, so he had a résumé full of embezzling charges. He'd reformed. He promised.

Although she wondered what Dick had done this time—probably more trouble with his probation officer—she didn't answer.

"Lizzie?" The secretary sounded even more panic-stricken, and she made a sort of gurgling noise. "I can't handle this stress all by myself. My throat is starting to close! And what about my heart condition?"

Well, *that* Lizzie couldn't ignore, even if most of the people in the office thought Yvonne's ailments—throat, heart, back, head, an endless list of food allergies—were about as real as the Easter Bunny.

It didn't matter. Yvonne was a hypochondriac and a terrible secretary to boot, but she was one of Lizzie's brood, and that was good enough.

"Yvonne, I'm here," Lizzie said soothingly. "Please just keep taking messages, okay? I'm sorry, but I'm just swamped working on the Christmas 2000 catalog."

Oooh, this was bad. First ignoring a plea for help, and now lying about it. She wasn't at all swamped with a catalog. She was sitting there staring into space, mooning about the wedding she was supposed to be in next week, the one with the really gorgeous groom and the Barbie's Nightmare bridesmaid dress and a whole lot of emotional confusion.

Lying. Ignoring. *Lizzie Muldoon,* she told herself, *you are going to hell for sure.*

"Lizzie, please talk to him," Yvonne begged, as her voice faded in and out. "Plus there are messages from Esmie in Human Resources that she needs another week off even though she was all out of vacation months ago, and somebody has to do something about GiGi the receptionist because she keeps calling us The Velvet *Pig* when she answers the phone. Oh, and another complaint came in about Oliver, the security guard. This time he fell asleep in the Dumpster, and the garbage guys found him this morning."

Lizzie wanted to scream. Didn't they all know she had other things to worry about right now? Okay, so The Velvet Fig—as opposed to *Pig*—purveyor of fine wearables and accessories, was *her* company. And they were all used to her as the chief mom and hand-holder around here, fixing mistakes, refereeing disagreements, covering behinds, soothing egos, offering a shoulder to cry on and maybe a raise or a vacation.... Could she help it if she was a sucker for wounded birds, stray dogs and people in trouble?

But today she needed her own hand held.

"What am I going to do?" she asked out loud.

"What?" her secretary echoed, with all kinds of static in the background. "I can't hear you! Don't tell me I'm losing my hearing now!"

Lizzie recognized the sound of it—Yvonne had her finger on the wrong intercom button again. "Messages, Yvonne," she called out, loud enough for her secretary to hear her through the door without the intercom. "Take messages. I'll get to them as soon as I can."

Lizzie frowned into space, putting Yvonne and Dick and all the other people at The Velvet Fig on hold for a moment. The charming little catalog company and its cashmere shawls and tapestry bags and chenille sweaters were going to have to survive without her. Because she had to leave for the wedding the day after tomorrow, and she needed a plan before that.

"There's no way I'm going to that wedding," she announced to the room at large, trying to sound confident and assertive. She crumpled. "But there's just no way to back out."

It was all she had been thinking about for days. There she'd be, in a horrid, unflattering dress, clutching some ghastly bouquet, while Eric Bellamy, her Eric, promised to love and cherish…Caroline Knox.

Lizzie wanted to crawl under a rock.

"Li-zeee!" a voice from the outer office called cheerfully.

It was too late to hide. Saffron, her best friend and business partner, came rolling in under a full head of steam, wearing a smile almost as big as the enormous velvet hat that tipped over her forehead.

Lizzie knew Saffron very well. And when Saffron smiled like that, it couldn't be good.

Cat. Canary. No, it couldn't be good.

"Wait till you hear *this!*" Saffron exclaimed, looking very pleased with herself. "All your troubles are over, Liz, because I've got it."

"And what exactly have you got?"

It could be anything from a bizarre new ad campaign for their catalog to a wacky new hairdo. With Saffron, you never could tell.

She sidled over closer, perching on the front edge of Lizzie's desk. "Well," she began breathlessly. "What I have is a way to make you shine. To make you glow! To make you a total and complete star in front of that stiff-rumped Caroline Knox and her blind, stupid groom."

"Are you going to tell me to get a tattoo? Or pierce something I don't want to pierce?"

"Of course not!" Saffron pooh-poohed. "Am I your best friend or am I not your best friend?"

"You are. I think." Lizzie preferred to reserve judgment until after she heard the rest of this.

"And don't I always know what's best for you?"

Now she was really starting to get nervous. "Spit it out. What is this all about?"

"The wedding. I told you." Saffron waggled her eyebrows just so Lizzie would know something really mind-boggling was coming.

Lizzie asked warily, "And? What about it?"

Her best friend bent in even closer, dropping her voice to a hush. "Picture this. It's the wedding of the millennium. The one where, in a moment of weakness, you agreed to be a bridesmaid in a hideous dress." She sniffed. "Pink-on-pink taffeta, littered with tiny embroidered swans. Good heavens above. The least Caroline could've done was order the dresses from us. That acid lime panne velvet tank dress would've *killed* on you. But no, she has to go and get some dopey, fussy designer who doesn't know butt bows went out with Sandra Dee—"

"I told you," Lizzie interrupted, watching the lights on her phone blink, wondering how she could gracefully get Saffron to get on with this. "We're too out there for Caroline. Besides, her mother would never let her use velvet or chenille or any of our other fabrics, not for a summer wedding. And certainly not our designs. It's just—" she shrugged "—not done. Not in her world."

"Well, ol' Genevieve's world could use a swift kick if you ask me," Saffron grumbled.

"All right, all right. Enough of that. For the purposes of the wedding weekend, we don't insult Genevieve Knox or her taste. Repeat after me—we love Genevieve."

"We love Genevieve," Saffron echoed, but she didn't sound enthusiastic.

"We love Genevieve as long as she's one of our major investors." Which was another reason Lizzie could hardly back out now. Was it her fault the only rich people she knew when she and Saffron needed investors were Caroline's mother and grandmother and Eric's parents? Every single one of them would be at this wedding, watching her, judging her, quizzing her about their investments, while all she wanted to do was sit in a corner and silently weep that Eric, the dream of her youth, was now lost to her forever. Preferring not to think about it, Lizzie tried to redirect Saffron. "Let's get back to the shining and the glowing. What's your big, amazing idea?"

"Okay." In the flicker of an eyelash, Saffron was back at full throttle. "Think about it—the wedding of the century, society reporters, photographers, movers, shakers, yadda, yadda, yadda. And you walk in, looking like a million bucks, making Caroline Knox wet her pants and faint into a heap, making Eric Bellamy *so* sorry he ever overlooked you."

Lizzie didn't know whether to laugh or cry. "I

appreciate your loyalty, Saff, but there's no way that's—''

"You didn't let me finish," Saffron protested. "Think about it. Caroline in a heap, Eric with his classic jaw hanging open..." Drawing herself up to her full five feet, Saffron whispered, "Because on your arm is the most gorgeous—''

"Oh, no. Not a guy."

Saffron crossed her arms over her curvy chest. "I know you're unfamiliar with the concept, but you must've gone out with one sometime, Liz. Let's see. Didn't you have dinner with a marketing rep from Yellow Jackets sometime in the fall of '95?"

"Very funny. But it doesn't matter. There is no way I'm taking a date—and a fix-up at that—to Eric's wedding." Lizzie busied herself sweeping a pile of pictures of crazy-quilted shoulder bags—projected items for their Christmas catalog—into a folder. "It's too humiliating to even think about."

"But that's the whole point, Liz—to spare you humiliation." Saffron pounced. "Think about how much more embarrassing it would be to go alone."

"You're coming with me."

Saffron rolled her eyes under the brim of that ridiculous hat, but at least she backed off. "Taking your best friend and business partner hardly counts. Come on, Lizzie. You know I'm right. And it doesn't have to be some weirdo blind date." She smiled sweetly. "Don't you see, Liz? That's the beauty of my plan—you can take Storm!"

Her eyes wide, Lizzie shot up in her seat. "Your brother?" she demanded. "He's twenty-two years old! I might as well be baby-sitting. Saffron, have you lost your mind?''

"What are you, ninety-five? It's a measly seven-year difference. Besides, he's gorgeous and he'd do it. I already asked."

Lizzie shook her head firmly. "Storm is very sweet, but *very* young."

"So he's young. It just means he looks even better on your arm."

"No way."

"He's a model, so he certainly knows his way around a tux. And around rich people." Saffron's eyes lit up with eagerness. "Come on, Liz—your beau Eric runs a magazine, and half the guests will be media types. Storm could use the exposure in front of people like that. And he wants to be an actor. So pretending to be your boyfriend—your very attentive and *lusty* boyfriend—would be good practice for him."

Lizzie started choking the minute the word *lusty* was mentioned. "Are you insane? Did you think for a minute I'd go for this? Storm? The Underwear Boy? Lusty with *me?*"

Saffron crossed her arms again, but she did back up, which Lizzie took as a good sign. "It's not very nice to call him the Underwear Boy," she said grumpily. "He *is* my brother."

"You call him that yourself. He and his under-wear—which make a very nice picture, I'll grant you—are on every bus stop from Chicago to Mil-waukee."

Saffron tipped her head to one side, spilling long auburn curls over her shoulder. "So are you saying you won't date him because he wears underwear for a living? I never knew you were such a snob."

"Please. I won't date him because he's twenty-two and he's like a puppy. I might be willing to get a cardboard box and let him sleep by my kitchen stove. But date Storm? As if."

"Well, you don't have anyone better to ask. You said so yourself." She chewed her lip, leaning over far enough to pry open Lizzie's desk and pull out a smiling photo of Eric Bellamy.

"How did you know that was there? Give that back."

But Saffron just waved it in the air. "If it were me, I wouldn't want to face Mr. Perfect without a really fabulous guy to sneer at him, to tell him once and for all, exactly what he passed up when he chose Miss Priss over you."

"I'm sure that would be lovely. But there's no way in any universe I would do that." Lizzie shook her head firmly. She might be a pushover at work, letting everybody in the place take extra days off and have long lunch hours, but not when it came to her personal life. "Not Storm. Not anyone else. I'm very happy going by myself."

"I'm not giving in. I'm serious about this, Liz. You need a guy on your arm. And not just a date." Her eyes gleamed. "A fiancé."

"Get over it, Saffron," Lizzie said plainly. "It isn't going to happen. Come on, pal. We'll have a fabulous time. We can have a slumber party and order s'mores from room service. And we can dish all the outfits, including the wedding dress, which I will bet you is a dead bore. Her mother said it was being hand-embroidered and beaded by blind Belgian nuns.''

She smiled bravely for Saffron's sake, trying not to think about how much of a pain this wedding was really going to be. ''So, do you want to drive down with me? It's at Lake Geneva, did I tell you that? It's hush-hush from the press.''

''Hush-hush? It's pretty obvious if you ask me. Swan's Folly, the most private, exquisite Swan Inn of all, is in Lake Geneva. Where else would Caroline get married, but at Daddy's best hotel?''

''It's actually Mommy's best hotel. Genevieve owns the place, lock, stock and barrel. You don't think the press will figure out where it is, do you?'' Lizzie asked in a sudden panic. ''What if they take my picture, you know, the ugly duckling bridesmaid? Or, even worse, mooning over Eric from some sideline?''

''That's easy. Don't moon,'' Saffron said sensibly. ''Look, I'll be there. I'll make sure you're not looking like a goon. Deal?''

''Deal. I have to be there by Thursday afternoon, for a welcome tea party or something ol' Gen is hosting. Are you driving with me?''

''Do I look insane?'' Saffron laughed out loud. ''Liz, we will be pals forever, but I will not set foot in that tin can of yours. No, I'll get a nice, big, fat limo. Driven by a very cute boy, hopefully. That way there'll be room for me *and* my luggage.''

''Then I guess I'll see you when you get there then. And that reminds me,'' Lizzie said with a frown, searching her desk for a small piece of notepaper with a phone number scrawled on it. ''That stupid portrait painter. You know, the one you found me to paint Caroline and Eric as my wedding present? He still hasn't delivered anything remotely resembling a painting.''

Saffron offered, ''I'll take care of it. I'll either pick it up myself or make him deliver it to the hotel. So you just stop worrying, and get back to being your usual creative, inspirational self, okay?''

Creative and inspirational? Like dealing with Yvonne the hypochondriac, Dick the embezzler, Esmie and her never-ending vacations, GiGi and her inability to form the words ''Velvet Fig,'' and Oliver the sleepwalking night watchman? Maybe it would be a blessing to get away for a few days, even if it *was* Eric's wedding.

''Thanks, Saff,'' Lizzie said, but her partner was already half out the door.

Saffron ducked back in long enough to say, ''No problem,'' and give Lizzie a wink. And then she was gone, humming a cheery tune as she went.

''Hmmm... She seems awfully pleased with herself.''

But why? Did Saffron have some other scheme up her trailing velvet sleeves?

''Nah,'' Lizzie decided, already turning her mind to Yvonne and the list of burning personnel problems. ''No hidden agenda. I'm sure of it.''

Thursday: Welcome to Swan's Folly!

WITH THE VELVET FIG miles behind her, Lizzie was feeling pretty darned good. She still hadn't come up with any solution to the Eric Bellamy problem—

namely, how to act happy at this farce of a wedding—but she couldn't be grumpy, not with the sun shining, a few puffy clouds in a carefree blue sky, and her foot firmly on the accelerator of her vintage Volkswagen Bug.

On a day like this, what could go wrong?

"Ooops." She was so caught up in her breezy drive through the Wisconsin countryside that she almost missed the nifty red convertible stopped by the side of the road. And there was a hunk-and-a-half standing next to the car, sort of leaning on it, looking like steam might come out his ears at any moment.

Without even thinking about it, Lizzie slammed on the brakes, veered off to the side, and shoved the Bug into reverse. As her car bumped backward over the gravel shoulder, she sized up the hunk in the rearview mirror. His image shimmered and shook there, not very clear, but clear enough. Dark hair, broad shoulders, sunglasses. Very cute. And very cranky.

Oh well. Handsome men were not her specialty, but she did know a fair amount about cars. Plus there was nothing like a good rescue to really get Lizzie's juices flowing. So maybe she could put a smile on that handsome face. Or at least get him to take off the shades, so she could see the rest of him. She smiled.

"Nice car," she called out brightly, unwinding herself from the front seat of the Bug, leaping out to admire his Porsche.

"Thanks." He stood up all the way, limping and then wincing slightly as he made his way to the front of his convertible.

Limping? Wincing?

"You aren't hurt, are you?" she asked quickly, hurrying to his side and offering an arm to lean on. "I just assumed that your car broke down. Was this an accident?"

"Naah." His voice was gruff as he brushed off her offer of support. "Old injury."

"Oh. Okay." Lizzie hung back, her hands in the pockets of her cutoffs. She saw now that he was tall, a good five inches taller than her own five-nine, that his hair was dark and cut short, that he wore a crisp white shirt with the cuffs hastily folded back, and dressy navy trousers. Under the dark glasses, his face looked attractive and appealing, with a strong jawline and an absolutely wonderful mouth. Right now his perfectly drawn lips were pressed together in irritation.

Good-looking guy, nicely dressed, Porsche... The Porsche wasn't new, but *still*. A rich boy, she supposed. His injury probably came from too much tennis or golf, or maybe even polo. And while she had nothing against rich boys—after all, her beloved Eric had more money than he knew what to do with—she had to admit to being slightly disappointed in this mysterious traveler. Eric aside, her taste tended to center on Men of the People, Regular Joes, guys who worked for a living. Okay, so she was an idealist. But she'd been brought up in a family chock full of them, and she couldn't help but look for kindred spirits, for the kind of men who believed as fiercely as she did in doing the Right Thing and contributing to the public good. Which rich men didn't usually have time to do. They were too busy hanging onto their money.

"You don't have a phone in your car, do you?" he asked impatiently.

That was a surprise. She had him pegged for the kind of guy who'd have at least two teeny-tiny, state-of-the-art flip phones in his pockets, with the stock exchange on his speed dial. "Your phone on the blink?" she inquired.

"As a matter of fact, yes." He scowled. "I've been here for a good half hour, and you're the first person who drove by. I'd like to call a tow truck and get on the road as soon as I can. I, uh, have somewhere I need to be."

Of course he did. "Maybe it would be quicker if I took a look, just to make sure it isn't something we can easily fix." Lizzie offered a soothing smile to her newest rescue project. "Do you remember what happened? Any funny noises or smells or smoke or anything that stands out?"

He just stood there, looking at her from behind those dark glasses, his arms folded over his chest.

Lizzie was used to this phenomenon, especially when it came to men and their cars. "I'm very good with cars. I promise. See my Bug over there? It's a '69, and I do all the maintenance myself." She widened her smile. "C'mon. Pop the hood for me. What can it hurt?"

"It's nothing you can fix."

She shrugged. "We won't know till we look, will we?"

He didn't want to let her under his hood. She

could feel his lack of trust drift over her in waves. Men. So predictable.

"Wouldn't it be better to let me try?" she persisted. "If it is something I can repair right now, you'll be on your way to your important meeting much faster than if you wait for a tow."

"It's not a meeting," he said grudgingly, although he did open the hood. "It's a wedding. A whole weekend's worth of wedding. I'm supposed to be at the grand opening garden party or whatever they called it." He checked his watch. "And I'm late. It started an hour ago."

"A wedding? You're kidding."

Lizzie stepped back. How many weddings were there that took all weekend and kicked off with a welcome tea in the rose garden? At least she knew her first impressions were right—if he was a friend or relative of either the Knoxes or the Bellamys, he pretty much had to be rich and snobby. The only person expected at this soirée who wasn't was, well, *her*.

Just to make sure, she ventured, "This wouldn't be the Bellamy-Knox wedding, would it?"

He looked her up and down, obviously taking in her casual knit tank top and cutoffs. "You, too?"

Well, she was planning to change once she got there. It was just so much more comfortable to drive in shorts. "Actually, I'm a bridesmaid." Saying it out loud still made her want to shudder, but she braved past it and stuck out a hand. "Lizzie Muldoon. Nice to meet you."

He took her hand in his, and she felt a little sizzle of electricity. And then he smiled, and Lizzie felt as if she'd been dipped in warm honey. Wow. He had a great smile. And then some.

"Joe Bellamy," he said.

"J-Joe?" she repeated. It hit her immediately. *Just a regular Joe.* And she couldn't help but notice that the warm, strong hand wrapped around hers wasn't wearing a wedding ring.

The thought popped into her head before she could stop it. *It's him! The Regular Joe I've been waiting for.* Except he didn't look all that regular. No, he was positively extraordinary.

"I'm a groomsman," he continued. "So who knows? Maybe we'll be walking down the aisle together."

Walking down the aisle together? Yikes! That sounded cozy. It sounded...cosmic.

She believed in fate—coming from her counter-culture family with its Tarot cards, astrology charts and crystals, she had no choice. If she wasn't careful, she'd start to think her destiny was bopping her in the head right this minute.

There she was, mooning about having to go to the wedding alone, and what happened? She literally ran into Regular Joe, he started talking about walking down the aisle, and he had no wedding ring. Talk about karma!

But then she processed the second part. *Bellamy.* As in Eric, the crush of her youth. As in Budge Bellamy, the Pretzel King, sitting on pots and pots of money. Every time anyone in America chomped on a pretzel, Budge Bellamy's cash registers went *ca-ching.*

At this wedding, with the same last name, Joe

Bellamy had to be related. Which meant he was definitely no Regular Joe.

If she could get her brain working—or her hand back—she might be able to think clearly and place him within the family hierarchy. "So you're a Bellamy. Are you a cousin?"

"Nope. No blood relation. Just a stepbrother. Eric's father was married to my mother for a few years back in the seventies."

"Oh, of course." Everyone knew that Budge Bellamy, Eric's father, had been married more times than Zsa Zsa Gabor. So this new Bellamy, Joe, fit in somewhere on the almost-related chart, a child of one of those extra spouses.

Lizzie shook her head, carefully extricating her hand from his grasp. Whew. If she wiped it on her shorts, would it be obvious that he had thrown her for a loop with his magic touch?

"I guess I'd better, you know, look at the engine," she said suddenly, backing up to the Porsche. "Oops."

She hadn't meant to fall over the thing.

Spinning around, Lizzie buried her head under the hood, but she couldn't concentrate. All she could think of was gorgeous Joe Bellamy.

There he was, standing behind her, staring at her backside as she peered at his carburetor and poked at his air filter.

Chapter Two

Nice view. Long legs, short shorts, curves in all the right places. Joe smiled, secure in the knowledge that his adorable Good Samaritan couldn't see the inventory he was taking.

If you had to blow a gasket in the middle of nowhere, he decided, this was definitely the way to go.

"Very nice," he said out loud, tipping his head to one side to get a better look.

"What did you say?" She bolted upright and turned around at the same time, her head barely missing the edge of the open hood.

He frowned. "Be careful with that hood, will you? The last thing I need is a woman with a bleeding head wound, passed out on the ground next to my car."

She gave him a frosty look. "Don't worry. I wouldn't think of getting blood on your precious Porsche."

"That's not what I meant," he protested. Actually, he'd been thinking about her seriously injured, him with a bum leg, the car out of commission, no phone, and no way to get help. But he could tell from the expression on her face that it was too late to tell her that.

She just muttered, "Men," shook the short, dark waves of her hair and dipped back under his hood.

Joe swore under his breath. *Women.*

His day just kept getting worse. He hadn't wanted to go to a silly society wedding in the first place, never had thought much of Eric's prissy bride-to-be or the rest of her family, and definitely didn't want to be stuck in a suit and tie all weekend. If he hadn't had this idiotic injury—a screwed-up knee from a freak accident during the Saint Patrick's Day parade—he might've been able to get out of the wedding.

Surely Joe, as an upstanding member of the Chicago Fire Department, could've begged off on account of work. Even if he'd been off the schedule, he could've switched with somebody, rescued a kitty in a tree, polished the truck, put out a few fires, had a great weekend. But *no.*

Just his luck he'd fallen off the back of a firetruck during the Saint Paddy's parade when he'd been stupid enough to try to eat an ice-cream cone and wave to a kid at the same time. Down he went, an old knee injury reaggravated, ligaments torn, and him forced onto medical leave. All of which meant he had no excuse to avoid his stepbrother's fancy wedding.

A Weekend with the Wealthy. The very idea made him itch worse than the cast he'd had on his leg after surgery.

But, hey, he'd tried to make the best of it. But then he'd gotten a bit lost on the drive up to Lake

Geneva, his car had broken down, and he'd had to sit and stew on a lonely country road for half an hour.

Could he help it if he was a bit testy?

Of course, the curve of Lizzie Muldoon's bottom in those shorts was a pretty good distraction. He narrowed his eyes. If she bent any further into the damn engine, she was going to split a seam. He'd pay money to see that.

"Hmmm," she mumbled, wiping her hands on the back pockets of her shorts as she turned around, her seams regrettably intact. Joe tried to pay attention to what she was saying. Slowly, she announced, "I'm afraid it's the fuel pump. Nothing I can do for that."

He refrained from saying "I told you so."

"You're going to have to get it towed to Lake Geneva. I'm sure that's the closest town with a decent garage."

Joe's mood darkened even further.

But then she gazed at him hopefully and asked, "Can I offer a ride?" and—even though he hated taking favors—Joe began to feel a whole lot more cheerful.

"I don't want to be any trouble," he said, as a token protest, but he was already limping around to the trunk for his bag. Take a ride in the country with a woman with a great smile and an even greater view from behind? *You bet.*

"After all," she told him, "we *are* going to the same place, and we're almost there." She wrenched the duffel bag out of his hand. "Here, let me. You're injured. You shouldn't be hauling that."

He grabbed it back. "I'm not an invalid."

She wrinkled up her cute little nose, as if she were considering fighting him for the suitcase—he could see the arguments forming on her lips. But apparently, she saw the look on his face and relented on the luggage issue. "How did it happen, anyway?" she inquired kindly, hovering at his elbow as she showed him the way to her trunk in the front of the VW. "Skiing? Polo?"

That got his attention. Who exactly did she think he was? "I've never played polo in my life. I think I've skied maybe twice."

"Oh." They traded speculative looks, as he contemplated how weird it was for her to picture him as a polo player, and she clearly tried to readjust her picture. "So how *did* you get it?"

"Work-related," he muttered, hoping to avoid telling her about the whole fire-truck-and-ice-cream-cone thing.

She opened her trunk, revealed that it was overflowing with luggage and parcels, absently shut it again, and moved around to the passenger door. Over her shoulder, she asked, "So what kind of work do you do?"

"Firefighter."

"Oh, my!" Now she regarded him with admiration and delight. She had the exact same expression his first-grade teacher had worn when he'd managed an A on his spelling test. "And you injured yourself on the job? Wow! That's so..." She wrestled his suitcase out of his grip again, and this time she hugged it to her front, brooking no objections. "So heroic! Wow!"

He didn't feel exactly right letting her think he blew out his knee fighting a fire. But it would be even worse to get into the embarrassing specifics of his parade escapade.

As he vacillated, Lizzie dealt with his bag. With an air of determination, she slammed the passenger seat forward and then pushed and shoved with all her might, trying to wedge his oversize duffel bag into the tiny back seat of the Bug.

Watching her, Joe grinned. Whoever she was, Lizzie Muldoon was pretty cute. It wasn't just her legs or her smile, although both were nice enough. It wasn't even her energy and spirit, although those were impressive, too. After all, she'd offered to fix his car, tote his bags and give him a lift. He had a feeling she would've carried him to the car if he'd asked. Or at least attempted it.

Maybe it was the way she'd looked at him as if she wanted to knit him afghans and tuck him up in bed with cocoa, which wasn't exactly what he normally did with women as sexy as she was. But, hey, he was game if she was.

"Maybe this wedding weekend won't be so bad after all," he said aloud, as Lizzie jammed the seat back into place and motioned for him to get in.

He eyed the front seat of her Bug doubtfully. A new wrinkle. How in the heck was he supposed to fold himself into *that?*

"Hop in," she said brightly.

"I'm not exactly hopping these days."

"Oh, of course you're not. Oh, dear. I'm afraid the '69 Bug wasn't built for guys as tall as you, especially not with the back seat so full." She put

an arm around him and tried to help him slide in
there. Funny, but it wasn't making things any easier
with her hands all over him, her soft breath puffing
into his cheek, her delectable curves jutting into his
shoulder....

"I can see this is uncomfortable for you," she
noted.

"A bit." Wincing, he maneuvered his bottom
onto the seat, wondering how much agony it would
cause him if he pulled her onto his lap. One thing
he could say for her vintage VW—if both of them
were crammed inside, it was going to be intimate.
He supposed he could handle a little pain given the
trade-off.

"This is terrible. You poor thing, all squashed in
there like that." Lizzie bent to guide the way, sliding a hand down his calf as he angled his legs in
under the dashboard. She rolled down his window
all the way and carefully edged the door closed.
"You know, you could always hang your leg out
the window, if that would help."

"You're kidding, right?"

"Well, no. I've driven that way before when it
was really hot," she said helpfully.

"You drove that way?" He didn't know whether
to be more astonished that she'd done it before, or
that she wanted him to try it now. He pulled off his
sunglasses and rubbed his forehead with the back of
one hand. "That sounds dangerous. Like, stupid
dangerous, not just fun dangerous."

She chewed her lip, looking at him with dismay.
"Well, you could always wait with your car, for the
tow truck, but I just wouldn't feel right leaving you

here by yourself. I could stay with you. Is that what you'd like?''

''What would I like?'' A stiff drink, a soft bed and about six hours to figure out what made Lizzie tick would've been a good start, but he kept it to himself. And whether or not he was jackknifed into a car the size of a peanut, there was no way he was staying there on that stupid country road one more minute. No way. ''I'm in now,'' he managed to reply, attempting to find some way to position his knee so it wouldn't kill him. ''Getting out again would be worse.''

''Oh, okay. Sure.'' She raced around to her side and jumped in. Just as he'd thought, with both of them in the seats, they were brushing shoulders, and every time she reached for her gearshift, she bumped his thigh. Not bad. As the Wisconsin countryside flew past, she smiled over at him. ''Doing okay?''

''Better than I thought.''

''Glad to hear it.'' Her gaze crept back to his face, as if she very much liked what she saw. As Joe bit back a smile, she asked, ''So you're a firefighter? Where at?''

He knew she was just making conversation to get his mind off the fact that his knee was folded into the dashboard and throbbing with pain, but he didn't mind. ''Chicago.''

''Really? I'm from Chicago, originally, I mean. I live in Madison now, which is great. Very laid-back and fun, cultural, crazy.'' She broke off, and her eyes clouded with confusion. ''Wait a sec. Were you coming from Chicago today?''

''Yeah. Why?''

"Because…" She paused, grinding her gears as she shifted into fourth. "Because if you were coming from Chicago, you were definitely on the wrong side of Lake Geneva when I found you. Were you lost?"

"No, of course not." He tried to straighten, but all he did was give himself a major, shooting pain all the way up his leg. "I was…"

"You were lost." Her eyes danced. "And unwilling to ask for directions, I'm sure."

"I was not."

"Just had a real need to go past Lake Geneva and come back at it from the other side?"

He could see the flash of humor in her eyes, but he still didn't appreciate being classified as a typical directionless male.

"Aw, come on," she kidded. "You'll get over it. Besides, I came along to save you, so even if you got lost, it's no big deal. It's kind of like karma, don't you think?"

"I didn't get lost."

Her smile widened. "But I *did* save you."

He supposed she had. His eyes narrowed. *He* was accustomed to filling the rescuer role, and now he found he wasn't crazy about the idea of Lizzie—or any other woman—swooping in and playing Little Miss Fix-it. It was unsettling.

She pointedly ignored his silence. "So you're a firefighter in Chicago. Cool. I didn't know Eric had any relatives in, you know, regular professions like that. I don't mean to pry or anything, but it is sort of different, given Budge the Pretzel King and Caroline's family and their whole hotel empire." She gave him a curious glance. "So does that make you feel, well, like a round peg at some very square family gatherings?"

Joe had never really considered himself part of the family, so it was a moot point. But he didn't mind Lizzie classifying him as different from the rest of the Bellamys, especially when it created that spark of interest in her eyes. "Oh, I come from a long line of round pegs. And is that good or bad?"

"Good," she murmured, giving him a tiny smile. "Very good."

He couldn't believe he was engaging in flirtatious banter while in pain and bent up like a boomerang, but it sure sounded like it. "Hmmm," he said, "you don't strike me as the square type yourself."

She shrugged. "Not in the slightest." Her glance slid his way. "And is that good or bad?"

"Oh, it's good," he repeated. He grinned. "Very, *very* good."

This time she laughed out loud. "Men. Always have to do you one better."

Well, *this* was totally unexpected. He knew there were lots of men in this world who loved going to weddings just for the romantic mood it gave all the bridesmaids and other fetching young ladies. Champagne on ice, misty music and lots of opportunity to score. Yeah, it was great for the guys who had "scoring" on the mind. Joe had always thought that was kind of pointless and stupid. If he hadn't talked to a woman first, if he didn't know who she was, why would he want to sleep with her?

So maybe that was why he was so surprised to find someone he liked as much as Lizzie Muldoon landing in his lap. He was enjoying the idea that someone as fun and unpretentious, as downright *normal* as Lizzie, was going to be at this society shindig, this wedding of the millennium. Even if she seemed an unlikely choice to be standing up for Caroline "Fort" Knox.

"So how'd you get roped into this whole wedding thing?" he inquired.

"Caroline was my roommate at Northwestern for a while."

"Huh. Never would've guessed that one." He would've figured Caroline would room with girls as starchy and snobby as she was, girls who would never think of wearing cutoffs and driving a wrecked-up old VW Bug to a posh wedding.

"Yeah, I know. It does seem odd," Lizzie reflected. "Believe it or not, because I am not at all sorority material, we were actually in the same sorority. My parents are major counterculture hippie types, and they were so ashamed. But I grew out of my rebellious phase quickly," she hastened to assure him. "As for Caro and Eric..." Lizzie drooped enough to look absolutely miserable. Barely audible, she confessed, "I introduced them."

"Not exactly an endorsement for the bride and groom."

More animated, she half turned to face him, hitching her left foot up onto the seat and driving with one hand on the wheel. "So you agree that they're a really terrible couple? I never did see what he saw in her, and for them to have lasted this long just *amazes* me." She rolled her eyes and let out a little noise of distress. "In a way, I feel like it's my fault because I introduced them, but good heavens! I had no way of knowing they would get together. I never thought in a million years that Caroline would be the kind of woman Eric would go for. Poor Eric."

He didn't think much of the happy couple, either, but on the whole, as trees and cows whizzed by at an alarming speed, he would've preferred Lizzie pay a bit more attention to her driving. If they crashed inside this collapsible cup of a car, his knee would be permanently imbedded in his forehead. "Umm, Lizzie. Eyes on the road, right?"

"Of course." She looked straight ahead, but she still sneaked him a glance every now and again. "Okay, so now you know my guilty secret, that I'm responsible for the two of them even meeting. Eric was in my freshman English Lit. class, and Caro was my roommate, and I remember it like it was yesterday—the scent of fall in the air, hurrying to class, running into Eric, hailing him, saying 'This is my roommate, Caroline Knox.' That was all it took. It's just so sad, because Eric has such potential, but Caroline brings out the worst in him. Now I can't help but feel like it's all my fault and I should somehow extricate Eric from what could be a terrible mistake. Am I wrong?"

"Uh, well, I don't know." What he did think was that her driving skills were not great, and that her loyalty to Eric, his ex-stepbrother, was a little odd. "As Caroline's old roommate, shouldn't you be on *her* side?"

"Heavens, no," she snapped. Then she seemed to remember she wasn't talking to herself, and her cheeks flushed rosy pink all at once. "I mean, of course, I think about Caroline, too. I worry that both of them will be unhappy. That's what I meant.''

Sure you did. Joe narrowed his eyes, deciding he had a pretty good bead on this.

After all, he'd hung around with Eric "Babe-Magnet'' Bellamy enough in his formative years to remember the drill. Women always fell all over Eric. And when the Babe-Magnet himself wasn't interested... Joe remembered quite well what they used to call "Eric's overflow." It was great to get a shot at the leftovers when you were eighteen, but nothing he wanted to fool with at the ripe old age of thirty.

Lizzie might be funny, genuine and bright, but Joe was beginning to see all the telltale signs that she was just another in the long line of women mesmerized by the fabulous Eric B. Too bad.

"Oh, wait, we're supposed to turn here," Lizzie said suddenly, slamming on the brakes and swerving onto a small gravel road.

Joe didn't have time to do more than let out a kind of yelp, trying desperately to catch himself as he was flung halfway across the gearshift. His shoulder and arm shoved into her, and his left hand slammed down between her thighs. *Uh-oh.* He found himself wishing there were better seat belts in old cars and enjoying the position, all at the same time.

He just let his fingers rest there, up close and personal.

But the car slowed and Lizzie delicately removed his hand, placing it back on his side of the car. "Sorry," she said with a funny squeak to her voice. "The, uh, turnoff came up a little quicker than I expected."

"No harm," he assured her. So why was he breathing like he'd just run a hard mile? And why did he have the overwhelming urge to slide his hand back down there, on purpose this time?

She turned her attention very pointedly to her driving, as the tiny car seemed to stutter through a whole series of holes and ruts.

"Ow," Joe exclaimed, and then "Ow" again, as he thumped up and down.

"This is the best way to get there, I swear. And we're almost there."

"Uh-huh." He winced, nursing his knee.

"Okay," she said cheerfully, steering her VW down the gravel road, changing the subject so obviously she might as well have used flash cards. "Now that we know what *I'm* doing at this wedding, what about you? How did you get to be a Bellamy?"

"I told you, my mother was married to Budge. That's all it took."

His tone should've warned her off, but Lizzie persisted. "But how? How did they meet? And get together? If she was anything like you, it seems odd she would've gone for that old bully, Budge."

Joe stayed noncommittal. This wasn't his favorite topic. "My father was a fireman, too. Died on the job. So my mom got a job as Budge's secretary."

"Ahhh…"

There was such a knowing tone to her voice, it took him aback. "What does that mean?"

"Nothing. I mean, it's just that…" She sounded apologetic as she explained, "Well, I'm sure you know that Budge is kind of notorious for marrying his secretaries.''

"Just two, I think. Yeah, well, whatever.'' He shrugged, wondering how to get her onto another subject. "It didn't last that long, and we went back to being poor and honest again, thank goodness.''

"Let's see,'' she said softly, as if she were thinking out loud. "Budge has been married a gazillion times, hasn't he? There's Viv, Eric's mother. I know her—she's one of my investors. And then there was the princess, whose name I can never remember, who had the dishy blond daughter. And now Mindy or Brenda or Candy or something. So where did your mother come in?''

"Wife number two. Out of five total, last time I counted." Darkly, he added, "But, hey, give Budge time. He may make that gazillion yet.''

"That's so sad, don't you think? That he's been married so many times, and the wives just keep getting younger? I'd really like to see Budge get into relationship therapy,'' she mused aloud. "He acts like a real bear all the time, but underneath, I think he has what it takes to be a wonderful person.''

Joe blinked. This was a little too touchy-feely for him. "I, uh, don't really think it's any of my business.''

"Even if Budge could use your help?''

"My help?'' He considered. "He falls into a river, he's in a burning building, I'll be there to pull him out. But otherwise, I think he's doing fine on his own. And one thing I'll say for Budge—he's up front about who he is—no phony baloney, no cheating, no lying." Joe shook his head. "If there's one thing I really hate, it's pretense and lies."

"Okay, well, that's true enough," Lizzie returned. "But I still say..."

He could tell she was ready to launch into another round of gooey stuff about Budge and his potential, and listening to it was going to be worse than the shooting pain in his leg. But then she spotted a new road, this one slender but at least paved, and she stopped talking long enough to hit the brakes, nice and soft, plenty early to make the turn quite neatly. She grinned at him, as if she knew he was bracing himself. "Better?"

Actually, he kind of preferred the first turn, the one where his hand ended up in her lap. He thought it was probably wiser not to tell her that, though.

She slowed the car again, pulling it up to a set of impressive wrought-iron gates with a pair of swans, beak to beak, worked into the design. With their heads together, they formed a heart. Above them, swirling letters formed the words *Swan's Folly.*

"I guess we're here," Joe said out loud. Beyond the gate, he could see rolling banks of green grass, stately trees, and a riot of thick, lush flowers sweeping down a winding country lane. It was beautiful, and it spoke volumes about what rich folks expected to see when they set out for a prefab weekend in the country. He hated it already.

A uniformed guard approached with a clipboard, and Lizzie gave their names. After he asked for ID and they each rummaged around to find some, the man dutifully checked them off his list and let them pass.

"Whew. Security's tight," she noted as they drove up the lane, past a babbling brook and a miniature bridge that looked like something out of a fairy tale. Beyond the bridge, cool blue water shimmered, and swans glided sedately around a small, immaculate lake.

"This place is so pretty," she murmured. "So romantic. So perfect for a wedding."

"Uh-huh." He surveyed the place with a cynical eye, noting that the shrubs had been clipped to look like swans and fanciful animals. Romantic? How about ostentatious, pretentious, even silly?

Joe leaned forward enough to see the main building out the front window. A huge, eccentric, rambling white country house, it loomed ahead of them, impressive, but wacky, as if someone had attached new pieces whenever and wherever fancy dictated— an extra wing here, a verandah there and a funny, squared-off turret in front. It had no particular architectural style; it just seemed haphazard and kind of loopy. No wonder they called it Swan's Folly.

"Isn't this place great?" Lizzie asked. While he didn't agree, he still thought the wistful look on her face was pretty appealing. As she pointed out details to him, exclaiming over every mullioned window and each topiary bush, she finally pulled the car to a stop in front of the wide, flower-lined main steps.

Joe frowned. "Hey, Lizzie, want to make a pact?"

"What?" she asked absently, apparently still basking in the aura of Swan's Folly.

"I can already tell I'm going to need an ally this weekend. You up for it?"

Lizzie gulped and gave him her full attention. "Sure." She sat up a little straighter, as if he'd just pinned a medal on her. "I'm honored to be your ally, Joe."

"Good." Joe reached for the door handle, only too happy to crack open his door and get the heck out of that rattletrap car. Once more on solid ground, with his legs under him, he tipped his head back in through the window. "Are you coming?"

"Oh, right. Coming."

She scrambled out and met him in the front of the Bug, suddenly all business as she set about dragging bags and parcels out of the trunk and piling them on the marble steps under the portico. Joe pitched in, unloading the back seat, and adding that baggage to the general heap.

"Whoa. That's a lot of stuff." Surveying the display, he wondered how the heck she'd squashed it into the Volkswagen in the first place, and what she was planning to do with it now that it was here. This was a long weekend, not a month in the country.

"If I can get the big garment bag over my shoulder, I can stick the hatbox under my arm, and then take your duffel bag with my other hand," Lizzie decided. "And then this one over my—"

"I can handle it," Joe contended. He kicked his duffel out of the way next to a big pot of geraniums, figuring he could come back for that later, and then hoisted a bulging tapestry case over one shoulder and a huge garment bag over the other.

"You can't do that. You're injured," Lizzie protested, grabbing at his shirt to try to get to the suitcases.

Joe took a wobbly step away from her, swatting at her hands. "If you think I'm letting you carry all this stuff while I tag along behind, you're nuts. What are you, a pack mule?"

"Joe," she warned, in an ominous tone, "give it back."

"Liz-zie," he said, mocking her by stretching the word out as long as she had. She made a face at him, and he just laughed in response. "Hand me that other one, will you?"

"No, I will not."

As he bobbed and wove, shifting under his burdens for better balance, she followed, both of them getting flushed as they played their quick game of hide-and-seek.

"Joe, put those things down. You might trip and make things worse," she tried, lunging at him. "Do you want to reinjure your knee?"

He stopped suddenly, swerving to one side like a bullfighter, eluding her easily. He was going to say, "Gotcha," until he saw her stumble on a step and fall headlong into Budge Bellamy, the father of the groom, the Pretzel King himself. Dressed in tennis white from head to toe, Budge had chosen the wrong moment to blast out the front door.

"Oops." Joe dumped the luggage quickly and limped over to collect Lizzie, who seemed to have gotten herself tangled up with the huge tennis racquet dangling from one of Budge's hands.

"Sorry, Mr. Bellamy," she said, awkwardly dusting off the front of his ample sweater vest.

"You two ever heard of a bellboy?" Budge growled, chomping on an ugly, unlit cigar as he took a gander at the scattered bags. "What're you doing, anyway—rolling luggage down the steps and seeing where it lands?"

"Hello to you, too," Joe said calmly. Although Lizzie looked anxious, Joe knew his stepfather's bluster too well to be cowed by it. "So how does it feel, going to a Bellamy wedding where you're not the groom?"

Budge made a harrumph noise, ignoring the jibe. "Good to see you, too, boy. But where'd you get the gimpy leg? What's that all about?"

"He was injured on the job," Lizzie replied helpfully. "You know, fighting a fire."

"I didn't say—" Joe began.

"Joey, Joey, we're going to have to get you out of that line of work. Your mother'd kill you if you got seriously hurt."

That didn't make a whole lot of sense, but Joe was used to that when it came to Budge. "I'm fine," he assured him.

"You look great, boy, just great." With the same hearty fist that held the racket, Budge pounded Joe on the back. "Didn't know you two knew each other." He peered suspiciously at Lizzie. "Old friends, are you?"

"Well, no, we just met. You remember me, don't you, Mr. Bellamy? Elizabeth Muldoon. The Velvet Fig? You invested in us."

Lowering his thick brows, he blared, "Sure I remember you, Muldoon. Glad you finally got here. Where's that partner of yours?"

"Saffron?" Lizzie asked with evident surprise.

"She's coming, but she decided to drive separately."

Only Lizzie would have a partner named Saffron, Joe decided.

"No, not the little girl with all that hair. I know her. The other one." Budge grinned, and there was a definite gleam in his eye. He waved his racket in the air, sketching it out for her. "The one with hair on his chest."

"Hair on his chest?" Lizzie echoed, looking totally baffled.

"You know what I mean." His intent was so obvious he might as well have winked at her.

Lizzie blinked. "I, uh—"

"Just keeping track of my investment," Budge continued, in the same smirky tone. "I like to know who's got my money, you know."

"Oh, oh, of course," she said quickly. "And I can assure you, your money is in good hands at The Velvet Fig. Profits are up, we're adding staff, we're thinking about opening a store in Chicago, and—"

"Yeah, yeah, yeah," Budge interrupted. "But I still want to meet the guy in charge."

Lizzie hesitated for a second. "But there is no guy in charge."

"Oh, hell, you girls are so skittish about shooting straight. At home, whoever wants to be on top can be on top—that's between you and him. But at work, if you don't want him to think he's running the show, just call him the vice president and get over it."

"But I don't have—"

Budge shook a finger in Lizzie's direction, once

more cutting her off. "I'm expecting to meet that man of yours this weekend, come hell or high water. You see that it happens." And then he started to stalk away, still chewing on his stogie, as Lizzie stood there, openmouthed.

"What was all that about?" Joe asked.

Lizzie just shook her head. "I have no idea."

Over his shoulder, Budge called out, "This weekend, Muldoon. I want to meet him. Or else."

And that was the last infuriating word they got from the Pretzel King.

Chapter Three

Was this a riddle? Or had Budge Bellamy lost his mind?

As she and Joe toted in their luggage, Lizzie was still trying to puzzle it out.

What in the world was Budge talking about? Had he mistaken her for someone else? But he couldn't have—he'd mentioned Saffron.

Saffron… Fake fiancé idea.

Lizzie was struck with a sudden panic. She tried to keep calm. Saffron wouldn't have. Would she?

"No," Lizzie muttered under her breath. "I told her very specifically not to."

Meanwhile, what must Joe think, after all those pointed comments about some mythical male partner who liked to be on top and should've been a vice president?

He seemed okay, though, still teasing her and fooling around as they continued their baggage parade. And Lizzie had to admit, it was pretty fun to walk into that fancy lobby with a gorgeous guy like Joe on her arm. She even waved to someone she thought she might recognize, just to be sure that at least *one* person noted her arrival.

As Joe went back for the last few things, Lizzie approached the exquisite, curving front desk, a study in dark wood and fresh flowers. "Hi, I'm checking in," she began.

She'd barely gotten her name out when she was greeted by an earsplitting shriek from behind.

"Lisa Malone, as I live and breathe!" someone cried, and Lizzie was enveloped in a bony hug and a cloud of expensive, cloying perfume.

"Lizzie Muldoon," she corrected, but it was choked off by all that perfume.

"Of course you remember me, don't you, Lisa? Caro's cousin, Petsy? We met eons ago, and we had the most fab time, all three of us girls. I'm a brides-maid, too, and aren't we going to have just the most fun?"

Lizzie withdrew far enough to get a good look at the person who'd accosted her. She vaguely remembered Caroline's older cousin, an insufferable snob if ever there was one, and definitely long past the "us girls" stage. Petsy was greyhound thin, wore her hair in a lacquered bouffant flip that was out-dated in 1968, and never smiled when she could sneer. Today she was wearing a short, flowered suit that looked like it had been made from someone's couch cushions.

She studied Lizzie's simple pointelle knit cami-sole and jeans shorts with a mixture of disdain and horror, rolling her pearls between her long, narrow fingers. "Lisa, you have the most interesting taste in fashion. You are just so...*you*, aren't you?"

"I try," Lizzie returned.

Petsy had already abandoned her perusal of Lizzie's outfit, and had now turned to the parcels stacked on the floor. She bent her twiglike body to poke into one stamped with The Velvet Fig label. "Did you bring some sweet little samples from that hobby shop of yours?"

As a matter of fact, Lizzie had come fully stocked with Velvet Fig merchandise, because she knew that the women at the wedding would all expect to be given gloves and hats and the signature velvet shoulder bags from the catalog. In her crankier moments, Lizzie even wondered whether the only reason she was asked to be a bridesmaid was to ensure a complete line of free clothes and accessories. Saffron was going to have a fit when she saw how much Lizzie was giving away, but what could she do?

Still, if Petsy expected to share in the bounty, she was going to have to behave better than *this*.

"I brought a few things," Lizzie said sweetly. "How distressing that they're not your style. You have such unbelievable taste that I'm afraid my little, uh, hobby shop just won't suit you."

"Oh, I know. When your standards are as high as mine, it's so hard to find the right sort of thing," Petsy said with a sniff.

Lizzie should've let well enough alone, but she just couldn't help it. Honestly, she couldn't. Not even when it came to Petsy. "You know, with your, um, slender figure, the burnout velvet swing dresses we're showing this year might look really nice on you."

She frowned at Petsy's unflattering suit, with its

puffed-up shoulders and wild flowers. And those scrawny legs... *Yechhh*. But, hey, maybe if Petsy changed her clothes and had a bit of a makeover, it would improve her self-image and her attitude.

Lizzie smiled encouragingly. "I'd put you in a longer dress, not too bare, something soft and floaty, maybe with a pair of velvet wedgies. And lighten up your hair a little?"

Petsy hovered there, torn between staying on her high horse and admitting she'd love to get her hands on the freebies. But she gave it up, letting out another high-pitched squeal when she caught sight of Joe, who was just bringing in the last bag.

"Hunk on the horizon," she stage-whispered happily. "Hellooo! Are you here for the wedding? Do I know you?"

The poor man dropped the suitcase with the others and then took a shaky step back, clearly startled by the outburst.

Lizzie bit her lip to hold back a smile. The expression on his face was priceless. If she'd had any doubt that he was a Regular Joe, his reaction to Petsy would've sealed it. "Joe," she called out, motioning for him to join her.

But Petsy cut him off at the pass. "I don't believe we've met," she simpered, holding out one long, pale hand. "Petronella Lambert Thorpe. Yes, that's right—one of *the* Lamberts."

"Sorry. I've never heard of *the* Lamberts." As he sidestepped the obstruction, he turned to Lizzie. "Have I?"

"Aren't you funny?" Petsy asked with a snorting laugh.

Lizzie explained, "Caroline's a Lambert on her mother's side. You know, Lambert Resorts and Hotels. Like this one."

"Oh," Joe replied. "Sure." But if he cared one bit about who owned the hotel dynasty, he sure wasn't letting on.

"And your name is...?" Petsy inquired.

"Joe. Joe Bellamy."

"Oooh, how *delish*. A Bellamy!" Her flip was positively twitching. Petsy slithered up closer, licking her lips. "You just stick with me, sweetie, and I'll teach you everything you need to know about who's who at the wedding."

Lizzie gritted her teeth. Bad-mouthing her catalog and her clothes was one thing, but now that the odious Petsy was moving in on Joe, Lizzie was really starting to steam. She thought it should be perfectly clear that Joe was with *her*. Okay, so they'd just met. But Petsy didn't know that.

"Just my luck," Lizzie muttered. For once in her life, she was starting out a special occasion with someone amazing at her side. And maybe if Budge Bellamy had kept his raving lunacy to himself, or if Ms. Super Snob of 1999 hadn't horned in, Lizzie could actually have enjoyed it.

After all, didn't Joe ask her to be his ally? That might translate into "just pals," which was where she always seemed to end up with the men she liked, but she'd had this funny little hope that it might mean something more. There had been a very intriguing look on his face, and he'd been staring at her bottom while she worked on his car. Didn't that mean something?

And then, when he dipped his hand between her legs on that reckless turn—*whew*. Lizzie's face flushed with heat just remembering.

Okay, so it was probably a total and complete accident and he didn't mean anything by it, and he'd now happily spend the whole weekend in the arms of Petsy Thorpe or Caroline's younger sister, Winnie, who was richer than Petsy and ten times as dippy, or someone even worse.

Lizzie wanted to scream.

As she stewed, Joe very carefully detached himself from Petsy and stood right next to Lizzie instead. That improved her mood. And while the desk clerk found their reservations and checked them in, Joe gave Lizzie a sly wink, as if to say, *Hey, we're in this together, aren't we?* Suddenly her luck began to seem a whole lot better.

Petsy wasn't going away easily, however. Sidling up on Lizzie's other side, she dipped her head and whispered, "So, is he The One?"

Lizzie gulped, feeling a hot flush creep up her neck. Had Joe heard that?

Was he "the one"? If she were honest with herself, she was wondering the same thing. But she'd only met him an hour ago, for goodness sake. She was certainly not going to leap to that conclusion just yet.

As she tried to sneak a peek at Joe to see whether he'd overheard Petsy's idiotic question, she could feel herself blushing like a ten-year-old with a crush on one of the Hansons. This was awful.

"Did you hear me, Lisa?" Petsy persisted, this

time not even bothering to lower her voice. "Is he the one your friend Saffron told me about or not?"

Behind her, Joe said wryly, "Come on, Lisa. Better fess up."

Lizzie was still trying to decide how best to respond when the desk clerk cut in. "Excuse me, Miss Muldoon? You're in room 215, in the east wing. Two of the bellmen have already started up with your luggage."

"Thank you," she managed to reply, taking the key, edging away from Petsy and her interrogation.

But the other bridesmaid just wasn't giving up. "Is this supposed to be a secret? If I had a fiancé like this one—"

"A what?" Lizzie sputtered, spinning back around.

Petsy blinked. "Fi-an-cé," she stressed, making it louder this time. "You know, the man to whom one is betrothed."

"I know what it means, but of course he's not my fiancé. We just met. I don't have a—"

But the clerk called out, "Oh, and your fiancé checked in a few hours ago."

Lizzie would cheerfully have sunk through the floor.

"So he's *not* the one," Petsy concluded, smacking her lips together and giving him the eye. "Aren't you naughty, Lisa, bringing this one along when you've got the real fiancé waiting upstairs?"

Just as Petsy moved in for the kill, a rather dirty toddler appeared out of nowhere and hurled himself at her skinny ankles. He began to scream bloody murder, effectively ending her attempt to vamp Joe.

"Lambie!" Petsy shouted over the din. "Mummy's busy, Lambie-kins."

But the child continued to wail, even picking up his volume, and Petsy eventually gave in. She lifted him off the ground, carefully keeping him at arm's length so as not to get grubby handprints on her couch-cushion suit. Then, with one last longing look at Joe, she marched off with her son dangling in front of her. As the child wiggled his legs and screamed like a banshee, Petsy hotfooted it out of the lobby.

Even in the midst of insanity and anxiety, Lizzie couldn't help but notice how horrible Petsy's bony rump looked in that outfit. "Be sure to come by and see the dresses I told you about," she called out. "I think we could do wonders for you, Petsy!"

The ungodly noise emanating from little Lambie trailed away, and Lizzie spun around to face Joe, back on the other track, the one with the mystery fiancé on it.

"Look, you should definitely know that I don't have a... I mean, I'm not..." She stopped in frustration, wondering how it would look if she just threw herself at his legs and started to howl like Lambie.

His eyes had a wary expression when he said, "You don't owe me any explanations."

"There aren't any. I don't have any more of a clue than you do!" She stopped. "Well, maybe I have one clue, a teeny, tiny hint, but that's all. But if it's what I think it may be, it isn't my fault, because I specifically said no, not in a million years."

Joe stood there, looking about as bewildered as they come.

Weakly, Lizzie added, "Honest."

He hesitated a moment, but then took her arm and nudged her past a curving staircase and some potted palms. "I didn't understand a word of that. But that's okay, because whether you do or do not have a boyfriend is none of my business."

"I don't!"

"Uh-huh." He shook his head. "Right now, what's important to me is that my duffel bag seems to have gone upstairs to your room when the bell-men carted away your stuff. So I'm going to have to come up with you long enough to get my bag back."

His eyes held her with a clear challenge. He might as well have come right out and said, *I'm going up with you to see whether you have a guy in your room.*

Lizzie found a smile for him, eager to prove to him that this burst of craziness was just a momentary aberration in a perfectly normal life. "You can come up with me. That would be great. For as long as you like. Because, I swear, there is nobody waiting for me, except possibly my business partner Saffron, who is very, very female."

And who had apparently been very, very busy, talking her little head off.

"How could there be a man waiting for me? I don't even know any men. I mean, what a scream, huh?" She forced a laugh.

But she could tell from the look on his face that he thought she was either a terrible liar or a candi-

date for the loony bin. And as they found the right
elevator, an antique brass cage around the corner
next to the hotel's old-fashioned morning room, she
couldn't let it drop.

"I promise this is all a misunderstanding. Budge,
Petsy, the desk clerk..." Set out that way, it sounded
damning even to *her* ears. She swallowed. "A co-
incidence or a joke or a misunderstanding. Something."

So why did she have this terrible feeling in the
pit of her stomach, centering on Saffron and her
studly brother Storm and an utterly insane idea to
bring the Underwear Boy along to the wedding and
pass him off as Lizzie's fiancé?

As the elevator stuttered up to the second floor,
Lizzie chewed her lip, her heart beating a little too
fast, her hands shaking, betraying her anxiety. If this
was Saffron's doing, if she really had brought Storm
after Lizzie had categorically told her not to, Lizzie
swore she would wring her partner's neck.

Aw, jeez. If only Saffron hadn't come up with the
whole thing just to make her best friend in the world
feel better. Even though Lizzie had expressly forbidden it, the idea still sprang from the goodness of
Saffron's heart. It was hard to be mad if that's what
it was.

She hazarded a glance at Joe. Should she say
something to him about Saffron's nutty scheme, just
in case? Did those beautiful green eyes of his look
stormy, or was that just her imagination?

Better not say anything. Not unless she opened
the door and there Storm was, in all his underwear-
model glory. And then she would say brightly, *Oh,*

look, Saffron's brought her brother. That explains that.

And that would be the end of it.

She played it over in her mind, practicing a carefree tone. *Oh, look, Saffron's brought her brother. That explains that.*

The elevator lurched precariously to a halt.

Joe folded back the brass door, holding it open for her, and Lizzie took a deep breath. With a definite feeling of foreboding, she stepped out onto the plush carpet of the hallway.

And almost collided with a tiny, elderly lady in a frilly lavender dress.

"Nana Lambert!" Lizzie said loudly, well aware that Caroline's eccentric grandmother was almost completely deaf. She was also eighty if she was a day, even though she wouldn't admit to more than sixty. She always wore pale purple, from the off-kilter swirl of her eye shadow to her tiny shoes. Maybe it was because of the shoes—Nana was fond of dancing slippers—but the old lady had a tendency to flit and flounce instead of just walking, which was probably why she'd run into Lizzie.

This time, Nana Lambert's deafness might come in handy. She was the one person who *couldn't* have heard any stories from Saffron.

"Hello, dear!" Nana shouted, and her chirrupy voice echoed in the hallway. "You're Caroline's friend, aren't you? The one with the little store?"

"Yes, that's right. The Velvet Fig. You invested in us, and we were very grateful." Lizzie bent to kiss the dear little thing on her papery cheek. "Nana, are you lost? Can I help you to your room?"

"Groom, did you say? Oh, no, dear, I'm not the one with the groom," Nana said with a chuckle. "That's my granddaughter, Caroline. Of course I've had my share of beaus since I lost that old prune Skip back in the sixties, but none I wanted to take down the aisle. Have to watch out for fortune hunters, you know."

"Nana, dear, I asked if you were *lost*," Lizzie repeated.

"Sauced? Heavens, no. I rarely take even a glass of sherry." And then Nana was off on another tangent, her gaze focused on Joe. "Do I know you? Oh, my stars! You must be the one I was just hearing about. That sweet girl with the odd name... What is her name? Parsley?" she asked vaguely. "Sage?"

"Saffron," Lizzie supplied, as her sinking feeling started to rise to flood stage. Not Nana, too!

"You must be the mysterious fiancé, mustn't you?" Nana inquired, clapping her hands together, and Lizzie let a little moan escape her throat just hearing that same blasted word.

Joe's face was hard to read as he bent down to speak more directly to Nana. "No, you're mistaken," he enunciated carefully. "I'm Eric's stepbrother. Do you remember me? We've met before."

"You say you're a matador?"

"No, he's a *firefighter*," Lizzie corrected.

"Yes, dear, I heard you. I once had a madcap affair with a bullfighter myself. But that was Spain, in the thirties, when life was so stormy and gay. Exciting man. Wonderful dancer." She shivered with the memory. "When we tangoed, I thought the world would stop. Ah, yes, he was exciting. But unstable. I'd be careful being engaged to this one, if I were you. Bullfighters are too passionate to be trusted.''

"I'll keep that in mind," Lizzie said under her breath, as Nana waved at them both and frolicked away down the hall, still reminiscing aloud about matadors and apocalyptic tangos under the stars.

Lizzie just shook her head.

"Okay," Joe said sternly, "let me tote this up for you. Old Mrs. Lambert, Pottsie or whatever her name was, Budge and even the front desk clerk all think you're engaged. You still expect me to believe this is just a mistake? Last chance to come clean, Lizzie."

"Well, it sounds like this may have been something my partner, Saffron, did," she said awkwardly, sure he must think she was certifiable by now. What was there to say? *My best friend and business partner is a total lunatic who has apparently been spreading rumors about me just for kicks?*

She couldn't say it. She and Saff had been partners and pals for six years. One didn't badmouth your best friend to a guy one had just met, not without being sure what had happened.

She couldn't even look at Joe as she turned the corner and ran smack into room 215.

"But this can't be right." She looked down at the key in her hand and then back up at the brass plaque on the door. "The Prince Siegfried Suite? I didn't ask for a suite."

Joe arched an eyebrow. "Maybe your fiancé up-graded you."

"For the last time—I don't have one!"

Joe crossed his arms over his chest, angling his chin at the door, as if to say *Put up or shut up.*

She had no choice but to slide her key into the hole, to hear the smooth click, and to ever-so-gently push it open.

No one.

"Wow," she whispered. It was gorgeous in there. Sure, it looked a little overstuffed, a little uptight, as if the queen might be dropping by for tea at any moment, but still very posh. And very large.

Lizzie tiptoed slowly past the elegant bathroom and fully equipped kitchen, very afraid that Storm and his underwear were going to pop out at any second.

No Storm. Her luggage was piled everywhere, but nobody else's, except for that one beat-up duffel that belonged to Joe.

She took a look around, taking in the cool green-and-cream decor, the lace and chintz, the delicate white furniture. In the main room, the parlor, there was a whole living room and dining room's worth of furniture, plus doors leading off who knew where on all sides. She supposed those had to be bedrooms. Two at least.

"I just asked for a regular room," she whispered.

There was also a sumptuous basket full of choc-olate and fruit set out on a lacquered tea table, and a silver champagne bucket chilling next to it. She approached cautiously. But the card propped up against the basket had her name on it. Only hers. She began to relax.

"Well, I was expecting a plain old room, but maybe since I'm a bridesmaid, they put me in a suite and sent me treats. God forbid I'm sharing my extra bedroom with Petsy or one of the others," she said with a nervous laugh. "But, look, no mystery man."

She spoke too soon.

The words were no sooner out of her mouth than one of the bedroom doors opened with a loud creak. She jumped, and Joe wheeled, and they both held their breath, waiting to see who was behind door number one.

"Huh?" Lizzie gasped. It wasn't Storm at all. Not even Saffron. It was a half-naked man daubed with all different colors of paint. "What the…?"

Short and slender, he wore tattered jeans and an earring in one ear. His vaguely blond hair was disheveled and standing up in a tuft on one side, as if he'd caked it with varnish.

Joe stepped in front of Lizzie, ready to ward off the odd intruder.

"Hello, love," the man said cheerfully, swiping a new streak of red across his bare torso. "I couldn't get any work done at home so I decided to finish the painting here. I knew you wouldn't mind."

And then he sauntered over to grab the whole bottle of champagne and nab an apple out of the fruit basket. Champagne and apple in hand, he strolled back into the bedroom, footloose and fancy-free, as if he owned the place.

"Zurik," Lizzie whispered around a throat that was threatening to close.

Joe sent her a very dark look, abandoning his protective stance. "So he's the guy, huh?" he asked with a definite edge to his voice. "I guess you go for the artsy type."

"Him? Me?" Lizzie gasped. "Uh, no."

"So, what are you saying? He broke in?" Joe took a few steps toward the bedroom door. "It'll take me about a second to throw the little weasel out."

"No, no!" Lizzie hurried to tell him. "You can't do that. Think about your injury. Besides, violence? I'd never forgive myself! I mean, I *do* know him. It's just..."

Well, what was it? Although at first she'd been so surprised she hadn't recognized him, it had only taken a minute for him to register. He was Alexander Zurik, the irresponsible portrait painter she'd hired to create her wedding present to Caroline and Eric. He hadn't finished on time, and Saffron had promised to track him down and get the painting.

"Zurik? And not Storm! Here I was blaming Saffron, and it isn't her fault at all. But what is Zurik doing *here*?"

She hadn't realized she'd spoken aloud until Joe snapped, "From the looks of him, I'd say he's painting. In your bedroom. In the buff."

"He wasn't in the buff. He had pants on," Lizzie protested.

"Yeah, let's all count our blessings on that one."

"This isn't what you think...." Lizzie was well aware she was beginning to sound like a broken record, but she was so flustered at that point she couldn't think of anything else to say.

Joe shrugged. "You thought you'd get away for the weekend, maybe have a little fling, and your boyfriend shows up unexpectedly. It happens."

But there was a tight expression on his face she didn't like one bit. What was it he'd said about phonies, about how he hated pretense and lies more than anything?

"You're wrong about this," Lizzie began, but she didn't get a chance to explain. She must've left the door ajar, because voices from the front hall told her she had visitors.

"Hello?" someone called. "Lizzie, darling, are you in? It's me, Auntie Viv. I've come by to stock up on scarves and handbags."

Oh, no. Not Viv. Viv Bellamy, the groom's eccentric, over-the-top mother, was yet another of Lizzie's investors. Viv loved upset, tumult and chaos. If she got a load of what was going on in Lizzie's suite, she'd be egging the combatants on, refereeing and supplying weapons, all at the same time. The last thing Lizzie needed was to involve Viv in this.

But it was too late to stop her. There she was, wearing a silk pantsuit with a cape, all in a blazing shade of orange that burned a permanent image into your retina.

Viv swooped in, all grand gestures and excited chitchat. And she'd brought the insufferable Petsy with her.

Lizzie couldn't take it anymore. She dropped into one of the pretty little chairs, one hand to her head.

"Joe!" Viv cried, running up and giving him a lavish hug. "I didn't expect to see you here."

"I was just leaving."

"Leaving?" Petsy echoed, bringing up the rear. "Do stay! We can model Lisa's clothes for you."

"I don't think so."

Viv actually pinched him on the cheek. "You sweetie pie, I haven't seen you since the engagement party, and then you ran off after about five minutes. I said to Eric, 'Where's the fire?'" And then she laughed heartily at her own joke.

"Viv," Lizzie said woodenly from her place in the chair. "How nice to see you."

"It better be nice to see me, Liz, honey. What've I got, a couple mil in that business of yours?"

"Well, yes, but..."

But Joe was making a beeline for the door, and Lizzie hadn't had a chance to explain.

As Viv launched into the story of how she'd run into Petsy and they both came up to see The Velvet Fig samples Lizzie had brought along, Joe grabbed his duffel bag and slipped away. He didn't even look back.

Lizzie was so numb from all the comings and goings and misunderstandings that she didn't even try to stop him. What could she say? *Through no fault of my own, everyone and his grandmother's uncle thinks I have a fiancé, plus there's this nutzoid painter I barely know half-naked in my bedroom....*

Naah. Joe believed in truth, honesty, the simple virtues. He was a hero, for goodness sake, running into burning buildings to carry infants and kittens to safety. Why, he was right this minute wounded and in pain because he'd charged headfirst into danger.

A real-live hero would not be interested in the bizarre woes of Lizzie Muldoon, Scarlet Woman.

Chapter Four

"We're just dying to hear all about this fiancé of yours," Viv announced, waving Joe out the door, obviously ready to get down to girl talk.

"There's nothing to—" Lizzie began, but Viv interrupted, giving Lizzie a friendly shove as she scooched herself onto the arm of the chair.

"Saffron already let the cat out of the bag, hon, and that cat ain't going back now. Don't be shy! You tell Auntie Viv all about him."

Petsy crossed her toothpick-thin arms over her chest and sniffed, "I don't think he even exists."

She was trying to be mean, but for once, horrid Petsy had hit the nail on the head.

"Sure he exists," Viv countered, "and I think it's great. You need a man in your life, Liz. Can't carry a torch for that son of mine forever, can you? Especially not now, when he's finally getting fitted for the ball and chain."

"Eric?" Lizzie whispered. "You knew how I felt about Eric?"

"Shoot, Liz, everybody knew."

Lizzie sank down even further, trying hard to ignore Viv's avid curiosity and Petsy's little snorts from the sidelines.

And then that damn bedroom door creaked open again. Still chomping on the apple, still half-naked, Zurik charged back into the parlor.

"Aren't you being awfully noisy out here?" he complained. "I can't be expected to work under these conditions."

After another pointed glare, he slammed back into the bedroom.

Viv's eyes widened. "He's a little scrawny, but not bad. And an artist—now that's interesting, isn't it?" Petsy just stood there with her mouth hanging open. Picking up steam, Viv continued, "Liz, honey, how did you meet? You've been engaged a while, right? So I guess he must be a real master, you know, where it counts." Wink, wink.

This was all too much for Lizzie. She stood up very slowly, very calmly. "If you'll excuse me, I'm going to get to the bottom of this. I'll be right back."

"Hey, hon, if you can get him back out here, I'd love to talk to him," Viv shouted after her. "You know, one artist to another."

Artist? Viv Bellamy did huge, bigger-than-life sculptures of nude men. *Very* nude men. If she wanted to talk to Zurik, it was to get him to lie down and pose, not to offer brush-stroking secrets.

"I'll just be a minute," Lizzie told the two ladies, twisting the doorknob behind her back, stumbling backward into what should've been *her* bedroom for the weekend.

With the door safely shut behind her, she paused,

took a deep breath and attempted to calm herself. It didn't help.

She sneezed, registering the fact that the exquisite bedroom in her exquisite suite now reeked of turpentine. He had taken the time to lay down some drop cloths, but there were filthy rags and tubes of paint everywhere.

The creep wasn't even looking at her, although she was staring a hole in his bare, paint-spattered back.

"Zurik," she challenged him, "just what do you think you're doing here?"

"Huh?" He daubed at a massive canvas set up on an easel near the window. Negligently, he glanced at Lizzie over one shoulder. "What am I doing? Shouldn't that be obvious?"

"I can tell you're painting, if that's what you mean," she returned in an aggrieved tone. "But why here?" And then she sneezed again, which sort of wrecked the righteous indignation she was trying to project.

This time his gaze was impatient. "I already told you—it was impossible to work at home, and I absolutely had to have a change of scenery."

"Yes, but—"

"Your friend, the little one with all the hair," he continued, frowning at his canvas as he worked, "told me if I didn't have the thing here by today she would personally carve out my heart with my palette knife."

"Well, I'm sure she didn't intend—"

"Cute girl, by the way," Zurik said thoughtfully. "Is she seeing anyone?"

Lizzie put a hand to her forehead. Saffron had threatened him with bodily harm and now he wanted to *date* her? She never would understand men. "Okay, but what she meant was that the painting had to be finished and dropped off by today, because I need that portrait as my wedding present to the happy couple. *Dropped off.* You weren't supposed to take up residence here, in my room."

"Oh, I know." He paused, scratching his nose with the hard end of his brush, negligently dribbling teal-colored paint in a thin streak down his chest. "But there was no chance of finishing back there. The muse just wasn't with me."

"You can take your muse and pack it up and get out of my bedroom." She sneezed. "Right now!"

Zurik shrugged his narrow shoulders. "Unless I'm here, painting away like a slave, I won't finish, and you won't have a wedding gift, will you? Besides, I like it here. The light is good. The champagne is excellent. And you have an extra bedroom. Why shouldn't I stay?"

Lizzie was familiar with getting pushed around by people. It happened every day of her life, what with Esmie and her permanent vacations, GiGi who couldn't say "fig," and Oliver the narcoleptic night watchman. They all took advantage—they knew it and she knew it and everyone else at The Velvet Fig knew it.

She'd tried to develop a backbone when it came to saying "no." Really she had.

Another hard sneeze rocked her whole body, and then her left eye started to water. It itched like crazy as she wiped away the moisture. Good grief! Carefully, she patted her eyelid with the tip of one finger. Was it swelling even as she touched it, or was that just her imagination?

"Besides, you don't want this room now," he said calmly, tossing her a glance over his shoulder. "You're obviously allergic to it. I'd get out of here and get an antihistamine if I were you."

"It's your fault," she snapped. "I'm allergic to your paint or something." Only it came out more like *I'b anergib to jor paib.*

"Huh," he said, totally unconcerned. "Well, I've got toxic chemicals all over. And I wouldn't expect the odor to dissipate for a couple of days. So, if you can't stay in this room," he concluded, "I might as well."

"Don't do this to me," she pleaded, but she already knew she was wavering. Her words were all clogged and nasal, her other eye had started to water, and now her whole face felt itchy and puffy. "Aaa-choo!"

"You have to have a wedding gift, don't you?" Zurik added. "And you *do* have an extra bedroom, one without the lingering odor of varnish or turpentine or oil paint. So what can it hurt to let me stay? You sleep in the other room, I stay here, you get a fabulous portrait of those two stiffs, painted by an up-and-coming artist who is a major bargain, and everyone is happy."

She reminded herself never to try to deal with artists. They were impossible. Unfortunately, this time he was also right. And if she didn't leave this room in the next thirty seconds, she was going to look like a giant blowfish, with red eyes and a blotchy nose and, oh, heavens, now her chin and neck were starting to prickle and twitch.

"Lizzie?" Viv's voice yelled loudly from the parlor. "Hon, we need to get going. You coming back?"

As she had to fight to keep from scratching about fifteen places at once, Lizzie made up her mind. Consumed with stress, hives, a skin rash or whatever, she was smart enough to know when karma and fate and destiny were all lining up against her. "Coming," she called back. And then to Zurik, she said quickly, "Okay, you can paint here for the time being. But you have to promise to stay in the room and finish the stupid painting and... Ahhh-chooo." She shook her head, trying to clear the haze. "You hab to probise *dot to cobe oud,* do you hear be?"

He nodded, already back into his artist's trance, concentrating on the canvas before him.

Lizzie backed out of there, more than ready to breathe air that wasn't laced with varnish and paint thinner. She shut the door, leaned against it, and inhaled deeply.

"You two not getting along?" Viv asked sympathetically. "We couldn't help but hear the raised voices."

Lizzie didn't answer—she was trying a few puffs of air through her nose to see if she was doing better. So far, so good.

Viv and Petsy had been busy poking through The Velvet Fig boxes and bags, and they had cashmere scarves and tapestry purses heaped on the floor. But when Viv looked up from the mess, she rose to her feet with alarm. "Good gracious, Liz, have you been crying?"

"No, it's allergies," Lizzie responded, scanning the room for tissues. At least she had her consonants back.

"It's okay, sweetie, everybody has these tiffs," Viv offered in a soothing tone. She draped an arm around Lizzie's shoulders. "But just between you and me, hon, you look like hell. I'd spruce up before I went down to Genevieve Knox's shindig if I were you."

"Oh, good heavens. The garden party." Still distracted, Lizzie surveyed the jumble of merchandise and luggage, wondering vaguely where she'd packed her own clothes, hoping the two women hadn't strewn those items in with the rest of this. "Do you think it's still going on? Is it worth it to try to make it?"

"It'll go on for hours." Viv rolled her eyes. "And you know how Gen is. She's probably hyperventilating already that one of the bridesmaids is missing. Better get down there and check in, or Gen will be so far into the sauce she'll never get out."

"You're right." Feeling miserable, Lizzie spotted the dress she'd planned to change into for the welcome garden party, and headed for the closest bathroom, the one attached to the parlor area.

She made the mistake of taking a gander at her reflection in the mirror and let out a yelp. She wasn't a vain person by nature, but this was ridiculous. "I look awful!"

"Never fear!" a carefree voice from the hall called out. "Saffron is here!"

Lizzie edged out from the powder room far enough to stop her friend in her tracks. Even if the thing with Zurik was just a misunderstanding, Saffron still needed to justify all the gossip she'd been spreading. "You," Lizzie said plainly, "have some explaining to do."

"Why?" Saff asked blithely. She tipped her head to one side, taking in her partner's appearance. "God, Lizzie, what happened to you? Don't tell me you stopped and rolled your face in poison ivy on the way up here? Catastrophe! We wanted you to knock Eric's socks off, but not from horror."

"Thanks for your vote of support." Lizzie marched back into the bathroom. She peeked back out, whispered, "Get rid of Viv and Petsy on the double. You and I need to talk," and then ducked back, where she splashed water on her face and tried to think positively about her appearance. Surely all the swelling and redness would go away soon.

"Okay, well, thanks for stopping by!" she heard Saffron say from the outer room. This was followed by the tread of footsteps out the front door, and some muffled goodbyes from Viv and Petsy. Saffron added, "We'll see you down in the rose garden, all right?"

And the door closed with a satisfying thump.

Half-in and half-out of the silk-lined, crocheted dress she was planning to wear to the welcome tea, Lizzie called out, "I hope you know, Saffron, that every single man, woman and child at this wedding seems to think I'm engaged."

Wordless, Saffron edged into the powder room

behind Lizzie and started to button up the cream-colored fabric.

Lizzie kept going, unwilling to stop now that she was on a roll. "I notice you're not even trying to defend yourself, and it's a good thing. Because now, not only do they think I have a fiancé, they even have a candidate for the fantasy man." As Saffron started to speak, Lizzie held up a hand. "I'm not blaming you for him, even though he *is* here because of you. I know he came on his own, though. But *still...*"

"Lizzie, it will all work ou—"

"Saffron, you should never have told these people that bogus story," Lizzie said sternly. "I know you were only trying to boost my image, you know, so that people would think I had a cool boyfriend and wasn't mooning over Eric. While I appreciate your loyalty, I have to tell you, it's turned into a total disaster. Now they all think I'm engaged to *Zurik.*"

"Zurik? The artist, you mean? Why would they think that?" Saffron asked, looking quite astonished.

"Maybe because he's painting in my bedroom at this very minute."

"Painting in your bedroom?" Saffron's eyes sparkled. "But that's charming. Does this mean we might get to see art being made, up close and personal?"

"It's not charming in the least," Lizzie argued. "It reeks! And it doesn't change the fact that you told people I had a fiancé and now they all think it's *him.*"

Saffron shook her head, forcing Lizzie to stand still so she could get the dress and the ruffle around the neckline adjusted right. "Let's talk about this later, okay? Right now we need to fix you up and get you down to that party."

"I can't go looking like this."

"No, you can't. Stay right there." Frowning, Saffron headed for her makeup pouch. As she dusted Lizzie with cosmetics, she kept up a running monologue. "I was down at that garden party—you know, the Welcome-to-Swan's-Folly tea that Genevieve Knox is running? That woman is a pity. I know you told me to be extraspecial nice to her this weekend, but she was really trying my patience. Okay, so first she's having a conniption fit because she thinks you're AWOL or something. She says she expected you hours ago, and what will she do without the third bridesmaid and yadda, yadda, yadda.... I swear, she needs a keeper."

"She has one. Her assistant called last week to see what time I was arriving. I guess they expected me on the dot," Lizzie offered, squinting at her reflection. Was her appearance getting any better? Sort of, she decided.

"There, that's the best I can do," Saffron announced, backing away, stowing her makeup brushes, and leading the way to the door. "I don't know what you did to yourself, but it seems to be fading. A little."

"I told you, it was Zurik's rags or his turpentine or something. My bedroom smells like the inside of a paint can!"

Saffron was way ahead of her, charging down the hall and ringing for the elevator, while Lizzie was still trying to juggle herself into her shoes. She had planned her entrance to the garden party—her first sight of Eric Bellamy in years—so differently!

"Will you hurry up?" Saffron demanded, pounding the elevator button a few more times for good measure. When it still didn't arrive, she took off for the stairs at a clip, pulling Lizzie along in her wake. "We'd better make tracks. Genevieve Knox is going to send out a search party if you don't show up soon. And the last thing we need is for her or one of her toadies to come up looking for you and run into the mad artist and his room full of turpentine."

"Too late." Striding ahead on longer legs, Lizzie hit the landing of the wide, curving staircase a step ahead of her friend. They moved a little slower across the lobby, trying not to attract too much attention from the other guests. Lowering her voice, Lizzie whispered, "Viv and Petsy already met him. That's why they think he's my fiancé. You know, the one you made up."

"How could I know they'd think it was Zurik?" Saffron protested. She held open the French doors to the terrace, waiting until Lizzie passed through. "I told them you had a fiancé because I brought along..."

Storm. Who was just now loping up to the terrace from the gardens below, offering his standard dazzling, brainless grin, the one that beamed from buses and billboards everywhere. He was wearing more clothes than usual, and he did look drop-dead handsome. Handsome, but vacant. You could turn on as many lights as you wanted to, but there would still be no one home.

"Hello, dear Lizzie," he declared, in a wooden

voice that made it sound as if he were reading the words one at a time off her forehead. "I have missed you since we have been apart." And then he grinned again, obviously pleased that he'd made it through his lines without forgetting anything. Dutifully, he leaned forward, pursing his lips.

Lizzie recoiled. "Oh, Saffron, you didn't..."

"Yes, I did," she whispered, elbowing Lizzie hard in the ribs. "Everyone but God is watching you right now, so play along, will you? Kiss him!"

They were all there. Every single person she didn't want to see. Especially one.

"Joe," Lizzie murmured. He was so cute, so real, so tempting, especially in the midst of Saffron's nonsense. It looked like Nana Lambert was trying to teach him how to tango through a clump of purple coneflowers, but his eyes were glued to Lizzie.

Further down in the rose garden, Budge Bellamy and his new wife were arm in arm, staring up at the new arrivals. Budge was still in his tennis whites, but he was squinting at Lizzie, as if taking her measure with the fiancé he'd heard so much about.

Behind them, Viv was turned away, filling a plate with tiny tea cakes, while Petsy chased after her son, who had scampered under a wicker table after a squealing little girl in a pink dress. Meanwhile, the hostess of this soirée, the oh-so-stuffy Genevieve Knox, mother of the bride, stood dead ahead, positively throbbing with anxiety. She was taking rapid sips from a china teacup clutched in an iron grip.

Neither the bride nor the groom was anywhere to be seen, and Lizzie supposed she should thank heaven for small favors. At least she would be spared the indignity of running into Eric.

But what about Joe? His eyes narrowed on her, and she knew what he was thinking. *You flirted with me when you had the painter waiting up in your suite. So who the hell is guy number three?*

"Saffron," Lizzie muttered, "I'm going to kill you."

"I can explain," Saffron whispered. She pressed something small and hard into Lizzie's hand, something that felt suspiciously like a ring. "Put this on for now, and I'll explain later. Right now, make nice and act engaged. I'll be right behind you."

She gave Lizzie a nudge, sending her tipping into Storm, who caught her nicely in his hugely muscled arms. He offered a polite peck on her cheek, awkwardly linked his arm through hers, and very carefully led the way down the hill to the garden.

Lizzie wanted to die.

"Elizabeth, dear, so glad you could make it." Genevieve Knox's cool, elegant tones did not disguise the fact that she was more than a bit frazzled. Not to mention the fact that Lizzie caught the distinct odor of Scotch emanating from Mrs. Knox's teacup. "Of course, we did expect you hours ago. I was getting quite anxious. We're already dealing with more disasters than I care to relate."

Winnie Knox, the bride-to-be's flaky younger sister, leaned in from the side. "Caro and Eric had a fight, and she went dashing off toward the gazebo, and Eric went after her, but no one's seen either of them in ages," she whispered helpfully. "So Mummy's upset."

"So sorry," Lizzie murmured, but Genevieve didn't appear to notice. Saffron was doing some kind of sign language, making circles around her ring finger. Lizzie got the idea and slipped the fake ring on her finger, and brother, did that feel weird.

"Eric forced the most unfortunate choices upon Caroline, in the wedding party, I mean—not you, dear—but the other one, that dreadful blond floozy, what's-her-name, the one whose mother used to be married to Budge Bellamy, who's traipsed all over Europe sleeping with Lord knows whom."

"Would that be Bianca?" Lizzie asked helpfully. She'd met Bianca whatever-her-last-name-was a few times, but didn't know her at all well. She did remember thinking that Bianca was an okay person, especially considering the fact that she was movie-star gorgeous, so Lizzie really doubted that the other bridesmaid had slept with anyone more than she should. But Lizzie supposed now was not the time to challenge Genevieve and her snobbish assumptions.

Too bad—Gen had moved on to other targets. Joe, from the sound of it. "We seem to have a disabled groomsman," she said woefully, "who may very well need crutches to get down the aisle. Crutches will mar the whole look of the wedding! It's dreadful. And the ring bearer is Petsy's horrid little monster... Have you met little Lambert? If that child bites one more ankle or throws one more Ping-Pong ball at my Waterford crystal, I swear I'll feed him to the swans myself." She raised a shaky hand to her silver-blond hair. "So, with all that going on, we can't do without bridesmaid number three, now can we?''

"I'm very sorry. For arriving late, I mean. I'm having a bad day,'' Lizzie managed.

As Saffron jumped in to assure Genevieve that everything was just ducky, Lizzie noticed Joe hovering over Genevieve's shoulder. He was eyeing Lizzie with obvious interest, his gaze skimming over Storm and then back to her, even dipping to take in the ugly stone now winking on her finger.

But it was interest of the I-can't-help-gawking-at-a-car-accident variety, not the I-think-I-like-you kind. Smoothing the short, dark waves of her hair with one hand, hoping her face was okay, Lizzie forced herself to look away from him, trying to concentrate on Genevieve's tipsy litany of woes.

Under the best of circumstances, she had trouble dealing with Caroline's mother. She knew the Knox matriarch did not approve of her friendship with Eric—ol' Gen had made it clear more than once that she thought Lizzie was some kind of threat to the whole Caroline-Eric thing, although Lizzie had never really understood why.

But she'd always felt as if Genevieve took one look at her and saw a scruffy urchin without benefit of breeding. Which was sort of true, if you thought about it. Not that Lizzie minded much—heck, she thought of *herself* as a scruffy urchin without benefit of breeding, and that was fine by her.

But now that she was very late, puffed up like an adder, and embroiled in what was turning out to be a major conspiracy to pretend to be engaged, she was even more uneasy around Genevieve.

Mrs. Knox took a good look at Lizzie's face. Her eyebrows shot up. "What in heaven have you done to yourself?"

"It's just a little allergic reaction. I'm sure it will be over soon." Unlike her fake engagement situation, which threatened to drag on forever, especially with Storm attached to her hip. *Oh, no.* Joe inched closer, ostensibly looking over a display of tea cakes at one of the lace-draped tables, but Lizzie knew he intended to eavesdrop on this inane conversation. He slid into a wicker chair not three feet away, and Lizzie bit down hard on her lip to keep herself from screaming or some other telltale sign of rampant emotional turmoil.

"Well, I certainly hope it's over soon." There was a twitch in the woman's smooth cheek, and a panicky note in her voice when she said, "The wedding is only two days away, and if one of the bridesmaids looks like Quasimodo, we'll all be ruined!"

"Quasimodo?" Storm screwed up his perfect face. "Did I model some of his new fall line?"

"Uh, no," Lizzie corrected quickly. "He's the Hunchback of Notre Dame."

He wrinkled his brow, thinking hard. "Oh, wait, I saw that. The Disney cartoon, right?"

"Uh-huh." Lizzie smiled tightly, envisioning scenarios where meddling, infuriating Saffron might turn up dead at a tea party, with her idiotic brother part of the same massacre. But first things first. If she didn't get Storm out of Joe's earshot, she was going to expire from embarrassment. "Storm, would you mind fetching me some tea and cookies? I'm famished."

He shrugged, straining the fabric of his jacket with his massive shoulders. "Okeydokey, um, honey," he added as an afterthought, planting a hesitant kiss on her cheek that was so transparently phony it wouldn't have fooled Little Lambie.

"Lizzie, you are so lucky," Winnie Knox cooed, giving Underwear Boy the once-over as he toddled off. "Your fiancé is *so* cute!"

"He's not m—" Lizzie began, but Saffron elbowed her, hard.

"Isn't he just a doll?" Saffron waggled her eyebrows, as if to say, *Look, isn't this going well?*

Yeah, it was going great. Right down the dumper.

As Storm concentrated hard to balance cookies on a thin Wedgwood plate, Winnie mused, "Mummy says he's an exec at The Velvet Fig, but I could swear I've seen him before. Oh, wait, I've got it. On a billboard. In his underpants!"

Great. The entire world had probably seen Storm in his tighty whities. She'd warned Saff that he was not a suitable fake fiancé, even if she'd wanted one, which she didn't. But she'd known all along that Storm was bound to get found out as an impostor, for this very reason. Of course the fact that he had an IQ of four was also a hint.

Had Saffron listened? Of course not.

"No one listens to me," Lizzie groused.

Saffron sent her a quick look, interceding on the double. "Storm *is* a model, as you've noticed, and he's also Lizzie's fiancé *and* an exec at our catalog company. Multitalented, that's our Storm."

Lizzie checked out the amused look on Joe's face, a tip-off that he had heard every word of that silly

résumé. "Why didn't you make him a nuclear phys-
icist and a NASA astronaut, too, while you were at
it?" she snapped at Saffron.

"Oh, Lizzie, aren't you funny?"

"Elizabeth, I really have to protest all the extra
guests you've brought," Genevieve interjected. She,
too, was eyeing the curves of Storm's muscled der-
riere as he tried to hold his plate level and keep little
Lambie's teeth away from his ankles at the same
time. "Not that your, um, fiancé, isn't welcome. Or
dear Saffron. But this was a closed guest list, as I'm
sure you can imagine. Every nook and cranny of
Swan's Folly is just full, full, full. Everyone in the
world wants to be at this wedding, including a whole
host of unsavory types, like those press people Eric
associates with, those pop-o-razzies or whatever
they call them."

"Eric doesn't work with paparazzi," Lizzie countered, as always coming to his defense. "He runs a
really nice magazine which I'm sure doesn't use
those people at all."

"*Those people* shouldn't even be allowed to live,
if you ask me, let alone drop in on *my* wedding.
And if they aren't bad enough, there's also some
sort of criminal running around!"

"Criminal?" Lizzie echoed.

"I don't wish to speak of it," Genevieve muttered.

Winnie confided, in a gossipy tone, "It's the latest
rumor. A jewel thief or something. Like George
Clooney in that movie. If you ask me, he can climb
in my window any time!"

"Winnifred, stop that drivel this instant. It's not

a jewel thief. It's an escaped convict or some dreadful person like that." Genevieve shuddered. "How dare this person, this common felon, barge into *my* wedding?"

"Mummy, it's Caro's wedding."

"Winnifred, be quiet. I meant Caroline's wedding, of course." She attempted to recover her composure. "Still, you must see why you should have warned us if you wanted to bring extra guests, because we have to be so very careful about each and every person on the premises, and now every room is taken and there's not a closet to spare."

"Don't worry. I'm sure I won't be adding anyone else." She glanced at Saffron with a touch of cynicism. "Will I?"

"Oh, my word," Genevieve breathed, trembling so hard whiskey sloshed out of her glass and into her saucer. "Tell me that isn't who I think it is, and she isn't carrying what I think she is. Anne!" she shouted, desperately searching for her assistant. "Do you have my pills?"

Lizzie heaved a sigh of relief, thrilled for the distraction, whatever it was. "Saffron," she whispered behind her hand, "why am I participating in this farce?"

"There is a very good reason that is too complicated to go into right now, but I promise I'll fill you in later." Saffron was trying to talk without moving her lips, and it looked and sounded ridiculous. "Listen, you said Viv and Petsy think Zurik is your fiancé, right? Viv is headed this way, so you might want to duck somewhere else before Storm gets back with the cookies, so she doesn't see you together.''

"I practically need a scorecard to remember who I can and cannot talk to!''

"Oh, pooh!'' Saffron retorted, dropping any pretense of talking quietly. "Listen—Viv and Petsy think you're involved with the painter, so stay away from them while you're with Storm. But Genevieve and Winnie are safe, since they think you're engaged. You and Storm, I mean. Budge is okay, too, since I told him about Storm before you got here.'' She screwed up her face. "Anyone else?''

"Don't forget Nana Lambert. If she sees me with Storm, she'll be convinced I'm cheating on Joe, the matador.''

"Huh?''

"Never mind.'' She silently promised herself she would kill Saffron the next time she got her alone, no matter what the rationale was behind all this playacting. Meanwhile, Storm was headed back with the plate of goodies, while Viv was zoning in from the other. And, worse yet, Joe was watching the whole thing.

Where could she hide?

"Oh, my God.'' Saffron stood stock-still.

"What now?'' Lizzie demanded, not sure anything could top what she'd already been through.

"Who is that blonde with the baby? The one in the little black dress.'' Saffron whispered. "Genevieve looks like she's going to explode into a million pieces.''

"That's Bianca, the other bridesmaid, the one Mrs. Knox hates.'' Lizzie gulped, not happy to see any human being generate that much heat. But a small, guilty part of her was sort of glad, because at least the brouhaha took attention away from *her* and her hot-and-cold-running fiancés.

"Who do you suppose the baby belongs to?" Saffron persisted. "It can't be good. Look how everyone has just stopped in their tracks to stare at her. She is gorgeous. But, good grief, you don't suppose...?"

"What?"

"The baby," Saffron said, raising her eyebrows. "Eric's?"

"Eric? My Eric? Heavens, no. Why would you think that?"

"Well, I heard something..."

"It's a vile lie," Lizzie insisted. "Eric is much too principled."

"Yeah, yeah, I know, the paragon of virtue. Meanwhile, who's that?" Saffron's tone was so warm, she might as well have said *va-va-va-voom*. "Is he cute or what?"

"Which one?" Lizzie inquired, trying to sound casual. She had her money bet on Joe, though.

"There are a lot of great-looking guys around here, aren't there?" Saffron was suddenly all smiles. "There's the cutie patootie up the hill talking to the blonde..."

"That's Eric's brother, Neill. I think he's the best man."

"He certainly is. Except maybe for this one." Saffron pointed a finger behind her back, right at Joe.

"Another Bellamy," Lizzie said gloomily. "Joe. The one I rescued on the way up here."

"You did?" Saffron hazarded another glance. "Lucky you."

"Oh, yeah, I'm *so* lucky. He thinks I'm a goofball and a liar."

"Maybe we should worry about him some other time." Saffron chewed her lip. "What is Storm doing with Viv Bellamy?"

Lizzie blinked, not sure she was seeing what she was seeing. Both had been moving toward her, but they'd run into each other in the middle. And now it looked as if the flamboyant sculptress and the Undie Boy were, well, flirting, teasing, touching, carrying on.

When Storm bent over to kiss Viv's hand and she giggled like a schoolgirl, it was hard not to miss.

"You know, I've heard Viv say a million times that anything can happen at a Bellamy wedding." Lizzie shook her head. "Now I know why. Good heavens. This isn't a wedding party—it's a circus!"

"How dare he," Saffron complained. "I'm paying him for this. The least he can do is stay on the job for five whole minutes."

"You're paying him?" Lizzie watched, open-mouthed, as Saffron stomped off on her tiny French heels to give her much larger brother a talking-to.

"Are you enjoying yourself?" a decidedly masculine voice asked at her elbow.

Lizzie spun around. Joe. And from the suspicious look on his face, he wasn't fooled by any of this.

Chapter Five

"Enjoying myself? Um, not really," Lizzie said.

"It looks like your boyfriend is enjoying himself. With Auntie Viv."

"He's not my boyfriend."

"Oh, that's right. You're engaged to the other one, the painter," Joe said dryly.

"Uh, no, not exactly."

"So this beefcake boy is really the one?" he asked, raising a very dubious eyebrow.

"Not exactly," Lizzie said helplessly, as Saffron waved her arms wildly from across two tables and a tower of tiny tea cakes. "Maybe. I mean, no. Oh, I don't know."

To her mortification, Joe laughed out loud.

Meanwhile, Budge was heading her way, thunderclouds gathering on his brow. At the same time, Viv and Storm sneaked off in the other direction, behind a tree, and Saffron threw up her hands and stomped after them.

"Muldoon!" Budge shouted around the cigar in his mouth. "Can't you keep a leash on that man of yours?"

She almost asked which one before she remembered that Budge was supposed to be in the Storm column. She wondered if anyone had a pen so she could start keeping some crib notes.

"So, what do you have to say for your fiancé? Not two minutes ago, he was making goo-goo eyes at my wife."

"He was?" Lizzie was confused. "Brenda? Wanda?"

"Rhonda!" he growled. "Not her. I mean Viv, my ex-wife. My first wife. Well, first and third, actually. Or maybe first and fourth. You know what Viv wants, don't you? To get that poor kid to pose for her, buck nekkid. Is that really what you want, for the man you love to be immortalized with his privates on parade?"

As Lizzie found herself struck with a sudden fit of coughing, Joe was helpful enough to pound her on the back. He didn't need to pound quite that hard, however.

"Well?" Budge prompted. "What about it? You happy to share the man you plan to marry with Viv?"

"Well, no, but..." But it was really hard to envision Storm as the man she intended to marry. It was, in fact, impossible. Finally, she had an inspiration. "He's a grown-up, so I suppose that's up to him."

"Ahh," Joe said from the sidelines. "An open relationship. How nice for you."

"I didn't say—"

"I don't know that I approve of those sorts of goings-on at a company working on my capital,"

Budge blustered. "We need to sit down and talk about the morality or lack of—"

This was the last thing Lizzie wanted to talk about. Thank goodness he was interrupted, this time by a high-pitched female voice, shrieking, "Lambie! My baby! Where is he?"

"Sounds like Petsy," Lizzie concluded. "Do you think she needs help?"

Joe shrugged. "Her kid shouldn't be hard to find. He seems to leave a trail of devastation in his wake." He indicated a table full of delicate sandwiches, piled high on silver serving dishes. "If I hadn't stopped him from kicking the leg, that whole table would've gone down. So he kicked me instead. And then he tried to pull Winnie's dress off."

But Petsy, the most annoying bridesmaid in the history of the universe, drowned him out, wandering closer, wailing even louder this time. "Lambie-kins, where are you? Where is Mommy's baaaby?"

It was only when Petsy stopped for breath that Lizzie caught the echo of a tiny moan. "Help," was all she heard. And maybe a splash.

As she tried to decide where it was coming from, Joe took off, sprinting unevenly past the tables, around the rosebushes, heading in the direction of the picturesque ruins at the end of the garden, what they called the Folly.

Lizzie could see that his gait was ragged, that he was favoring his right knee. "Joe, you shouldn't be running!" He didn't stop. So she had no choice— she ran after him, all the way to the swan pond on the other side of the Folly.

There was Lambie all right, up to his neck in crystal-blue water, holding up one small, pale hand. Her heart pounding, Lizzie arrived at the edge of the water just as Joe leapt into the lake in one fluid motion, intent on saving the boy.

Except the water was only a foot and a half deep.

Joe landed very badly. He cried out in pain, grabbing his injured knee as he fell clumsily onto one side.

A small girl with curly hair, apparently Lambie's accomplice in this nasty little game, laughed hysterically, rolling her flouncy pink dress around on the grass, while the rotten tot unfolded himself and bounced up, chortling, "Ha ha! I fooled you!"

"You kids are in big trouble! You could've killed someone. Get away from the water immediately."

Lizzie felt like throttling both of them, but her first priority was Joe, who had once more charged into danger without regard for his personal safety. Wow. What a great guy.

"Joe?" she called, hesitating where she stood on the grass. "Are you okay?"

His only answer was a grimace, as he gripped his knee. And suddenly a pair of swans veered closer, honking and snapping their long, scary beaks. Without even thinking, Lizzie waded in to rescue Joe.

The water was colder than it looked, and even though it barely hit her knees, she'd managed to drench her dress all the way up to her thighs by the time she'd taken two steps. The crocheted fabric weighed a ton, and it was amazingly uncomfortable, rubbing against her as she staggered through the water. Not only that, but the bottom of the lake was slippery and tough to negotiate. She kicked off her shoes and kept going.

"Shoo, shoo," she said to the swans, waving her arms at them. How bizarre. They did as they were told, scattering back to the far side of the lagoon. If only the children were as easy to control.

Joe reached for her. "Lizzie…"

"Don't worry. I'll get you out," she murmured, propping him up in her lap to keep his head above the water while she figured this out.

"I'm in no danger of drowning," he said with a scowl. But he left his head in the curve of her arm just the same.

His jaw felt rigid under her hand, and his lips were very close to hers. Very close and very sexy, even twisted into such a fierce expression. She had the oddest notion that it might make them both feel better if she just bent down and kissed him. For a long time.

Honk, honk. Lambie and his pal did harmony with the geese, yelling, "Look, look, they're going to kiss! Eeeuw!"

Wrapping Joe in a protective embrace, Lizzie stroked his head as she glared at the little beasts.

"Look, I appreciate your help," Joe muttered, "but I don't want to be petted. I want to get out of here."

"Here," she tried, "loop your arm over here. Maybe if you lean on me."

Ooops. When he transferred his weight to her, she did her best to hold him up, but it felt as if she were trying to lift a tugboat over her head. All she did was lose her footing and topple them both. *Sploosh.*

Joe landed on his back, with her flat along the front of him.

Now she was totally and completely wet. If her dress soaked up any more water, there wouldn't be any left in the pond.

Dazed, Lizzie lifted her head and gazed straight into his pained, amused eyes. *Oh, my.* She felt her face flush hot, even under the cool splash of lake water.

This was cozy. As they grappled to find leverage, her dress got wadded up into one big lump of wet crochet, and one of his hands formed a very intimate bond with the round curve of her bottom.

"Wait," she said breathlessly, but she surged against him at the same time he sat up, which meant his grip on her backside tightened, and her breasts bumped right up under his nose.

His voice was rough when he whispered, "Just sit still and don't move."

Oh, she wasn't planning on moving. Not in this position. With a sopping wet dress and a warm, breathing man plastered to the front of it, she was in a very precarious place.

"Uh, Joe..." Her voice came out squeaky and weird. "Could you move your, you know..."

"My hand?"

"The one on my..."

He removed it. Delicately, Lizzie peeled away from him. After a long pause to try to get her heart back to a more normal rhythm, she decided to try again.

She crouched behind him, wobbly but determined to avoid any more underwater Greco-Roman wrestling. "Come on. I'll pull, and you push with your good leg, and we'll get out of this stupid lake."

It wasn't pretty, but it worked.

"W-we did it." By the time she had him out of there, her breath was coming in huge, shaky gulps, and she sort of collapsed against him.

Joe gritted his teeth so hard she could hear it. "I may never use this leg again."

Lizzie felt laughter bubbling up inside her. It was totally inappropriate, but there it was. Weakly, she tipped her forehead against his collarbone, and his arms came around her automatically.

"Lizzie," he whispered, pulling up his good knee and bracing her against it. "Another rescue, huh?" With one finger, he brushed back a strand of wet hair at her temple. "What am I going to do with you?"

"Well, you could..." *Kiss me,* she added silently.

Joe bent closer, his lips a fraction of an inch away. Warm, soft, wet... Lizzie's breath caught in her throat, she closed her eyes, and she lifted herself up for the kiss.

The words "Holy hell!" came blasting right between them in Budge Bellamy's distinctive roar.

Lizzie jumped back, Joe yelped, "Ow! You're on my knee," and the moment was lost forever.

Yep, it was Budge all right, marching up to the swan pond with his newest wife, Brenda or Wanda or whatever her name was.

The wife gasped, "Look at that, Budge, and in front of the children. Fawn, get over here." She snatched up the little girl in the pink dress and covered her eyes, as if to shield her from the smut in the grass.

"Mommy, Mommy," Fawn wailed, "Lambie ranned in and pretended to be drownding and the man came to get him but he fell and it was sooo funny. Lambie ran away, though, but I stayed."

"It's okay, Fawn, honey. You're safe now," her mother murmured.

Safe? It was on the tip of Lizzie's tongue to tell Budge and his silly bride that this was partly their precious daughter's fault. But she kept her mouth shut. With her crocheted dress molded to her body like a wetsuit, she was in no position to call attention to herself. So she basically just cowered behind Joe, trying to pluck her dress away from her body and flap it in the breeze.

"Joey, I'm surprised at you," Budge bellowed. "Get away from that girl. Don't you know she's taken? And you, Muldoon, no wonder your boyfriend's eye is wandering. You listen to me—it's bad business to cheat on your partner."

That was rich, coming from a man who'd been married a gazillion times.

"You try to dump Storm," Budge warned, "and he'll walk away with half your business."

"I'll, uh, keep that in mind," Lizzie said darkly.

Joe gave her a dirty look. She didn't really understand why, but she had a feeling it had something to do with Storm and this half-witted fiancé game.

"Come on, Budge. Fawn's dress is filthy. Let's get her back to the room and changed," urged Sandy or Linda or whatever her name was. Still muttering under his breath about Lizzie's folly, Budge allowed his wife to pull him away.

Lizzie felt like screaming with frustration. Instead, she cursed out loud as she stood up, and then offered Joe a hand.

He took it.

"Are you okay?" she asked, unable to miss the distress signals he was giving out. There was a white edge of pain around his mouth every time he moved a muscle.

He pulled himself to his feet, stood very still for a second, as if testing his balance, and then immediately began to unbutton his shirt.

Okay, this was surprising. "What are you doing that for?"

His eyes narrowed. "Because I don't think you want to walk all the way back up to the hotel in a transparent dress."

Lizzie stiffened. Slowly, she peeked down at the front of her. "Oh, my." She swallowed. She crossed her arms over her chest. Waterlogged crochet didn't hide much, did it?

"Where are your shoes?"

"Um, in the lake," she said faintly.

Joe considered. "I say we leave 'em."

"Okay by me."

He held out the shirt and she took it without a word of protest. This was not the time to stand on ceremony. My, but Joe had a nice chest, all exposed that way. Her fingers were uncoordinated as she tried to slip the damp shirt on over her shoulders, and she found herself staring at that smooth, muscled skin, all hard and angled in just the right places.

She licked her lips.

Joe drew closer, grabbing the edges of the shirt in his fists, jerking Lizzie up to meet his intense gaze. She held herself very still.

"There is no way in hell," Joe whispered, "I would ever believe you were in love with that hunk of sculptured lard."

"You mean St—" she began, but then he kissed her.

It was harsh and angry and a little chilly, what with all the wet fabric between them, but Lizzie didn't care. She wrapped her arms around his bare flesh and held on for dear life. And when he dropped her, gasping for breath, she wished he would start again right now.

But without another word, Joe spun away. Skirting behind the Folly, he limped off in the opposite direction.

"Where are you going?" she called. "The hotel is back that way."

"I'm in one of the cottages. Thistledown or something." He hooked his thumb. "Out on the back forty."

"See you later," she yelled. "Okay?"

But Joe didn't answer. *There is no way in hell I would ever believe you were in love with that hunk of sculptured lard.*

And why did that thought make her so darn happy?

Shivering under Joe's soggy shirt and her own droopy dress, Lizzie hiked back up to that ill-fated afternoon tea, where everything that could go wrong already had. But several guests were still hanging on, Saffron among them.

From behind a towering oak tree, Lizzie hissed, "Pssst, Saffron, over here."

Her friend's eyes widened, and she scooted over there on the double. "What happened to you?" she cried, tugging at Lizzie's sleeve with distaste, pulling her even further back into the shadow of the tree where other guests were unlikely to see them. She cast a glance at Lizzie's dripping hem and bare feet. "I leave you alone for five minutes and you fall in a lake? And whose shirt are you wearing?"

Lizzie lifted her chin, tossing back her drooping hair. "I didn't fall. I jumped in. To save Joe. He gave me his shirt."

Saffron pressed her lips together. "Uh-huh. You saved him? From what? A six-inch undertow? Maybe a runaway swan?"

"Actually, I saved him from that little rat Lambie, who pretended he was going down for the third time." She frowned. "After that performance, I'll volunteer to drown the brat myself."

"I can't believe I'm hearing this. Lizzie Muldoon, threatening to drown a four-year-old. Are you sure you don't think he can be redeemed if you could only get him onto a macrobiotic diet?" Saffron teased. "Or maybe into a nurturing playgroup for troubled toddlers?"

"Well, I do think even Lambie could be saved given the right sort of supervision. But short-term, I'd rather shake him."

"I'm shocked. That doesn't sound like you."

"When my best friend makes me lie through my

teeth to groups of ten or more, I tend to get testy,'' Lizzie returned. Grimly, she regarded Saffron. ''The jig is up, Saff. I need to know why in the world you told everyone that I was engaged to your brother. Now.''

Saffron opened her mouth, closed it again, and began to beat a hasty retreat. ''You know, I should really find Storm. You never know—''

''He's fine.'' Resolute, Lizzie caught her friend's hand and yanked her back to face the music. ''He's probably stripped to his skivvies and flexing his pecs for Viv, even as we speak.''

''But that will screw up everything,'' Saffron protested.

''You should've thought of that before you started this nonsense.''

''So you're holding me prisoner in the middle of the forest?'' Saffron pretended to be outraged. ''Can't we at least take this upstairs?'' She wrinkled her nose. ''You can change your clothes before you put my feet to the fire.''

''Good idea. Feet to the fire, I mean. I like that.'' Tired of standing in a puddle, Lizzie led through the trees and in a back door to the east wing of the hotel. ''This way.''

Saffron didn't look happy, but she went along with it. ''If I agree to discuss this, do you promise to keep an open mind?''

''No, I'm not promising anything.''

Lizzie tiptoed up the back stairs, skulking around as if she were the mysterious cat burglar Winnie had mentioned earlier. God forbid anyone should see her

like this, or ask pressing questions about her love
life with Storm or Zurik or Joe the matador.

It was just too distressing.

As she fished around in her pocket for her room
key, thankful it had survived her dip in the pond,
she inquired, "Why do we have a suite, anyway? Is
that something else you did?"

"Uh-huh." Saffron smiled. "When I called last
week to check on the accommodations, I upgraded
us. I ordered champagne and chocolate, too. I just
thought, might as well be comfy, right?"

"I suppose." Safely inside, Lizzie looked around
for more surprises. She could hear Zurik in bedroom
number one, swearing and bashing around. At least
she hoped that was Zurik. Finding nothing else unexpected, she went to work on her garment bag to
locate an outfit to change into. "You wait right
here," she ordered Saffron. "I'll just change in my
room and come right back."

"Your room?" Saffron trailed after her. "But
that's my—"

Once inside the second bedroom, Lizzie knew immediately that something didn't add up. It was a
pretty, spacious room, with two double beds, a big
armoire, a closet and a bathroom, and the same attention to luxury as the rest of the suite. It was also
jam-packed with trunks and bags, piled sky-high.

Saffron often traveled with lots of luggage, but
this was ridiculous. "Whose is all this?" Lizzie demanded.

"Mine. And Storm's. It takes a lot of wardrobe
to pull off a weekend like this."

"And where is Storm expecting to sleep?" Lizzie

asked, doing the math on how many beds and how many people were combined in the Prince Siegfried Suite.

"Here." Saffron shrugged. "There are two beds and he *is* my brother. I don't mind."

Lizzie crossed her arms over her chest, starting to get a very bad feeling about this. "And what about me?"

"Hmmm... Oh, you mean with Zurik in the other one. This is a dilemma. I know! You can sleep on the sofa bed in the parlor."

Saffron announced it as if it were a real brainstorm. Lizzie didn't quite see it that way.

She was a guest at the wedding of the millennium, she was a bridesmaid, she was paying for a luxurious two-bedroom suite, and she was supposed to bunk on a pullout bed in the parlor?

"Why can't Storm take the sofa?" she argued. "I'll share the double room with you."

"Lizzie, Lizzie, Lizzie," Saffron pooh-poohed, as she started unpacking her suitcases and putting away her things. "You know Storm likes to walk around in his undies. And he sleeps in the nude. I'm his sister, I'm used to it. But I don't think you want him sprawled there in the living room..."

"Oh, good grief." She could just imagine Storm in his tiny briefs or, God forbid, with his "privates on parade," as Budge put it, while Viv and Genevieve and Winnie all came traipsing through looking for freebies, or Joe walked in, looking for Lizzie.... She cringed. It was unthinkable. Horrifying.

"What did I do to deserve this?" Lizzie whispered.

"Oh, come on, it'll be fun," Saffron said gaily. "Like a big slumber party. Lucky I changed us to a suite, isn't it?"

"Lucky? You think any of this is lucky? I think it's insane!"

"Lizzie, calm down." Saffron switched to Lizzie's luggage, digging out a bright cotton T-shirt and a pair of jeans. "Here, take these. And comb your hair. You'll feel better."

"I'll feel better? Are you nuts?" She took a deep breath, but it didn't help. "I am at a wedding I didn't want to go to in the first place, the only man I used to think I would ever love is getting married in two days, all of the investors of my poor company are here watching me, I've met a man I like and he thinks I'm nuts, and all the other people here think I'm attached to three different men! How can I feel better?"

"If you're dry?" Saffron ventured.

Swearing something really vile, Lizzie stormed into the bathroom and shed her wet clothes. But her mood softened as she stood there, fingering Joe's shirt. Wasn't that sweet, how he'd offered his shirt? And wasn't it even sweeter, how he'd kissed her like there was no tomorrow? *Yum.*

"Lizzie? Are you coming out sometime today?" Saffron called. "I need to unpack my toiletries in that bathroom."

That brought her up short. Saffron and her toiletries, Storm and his underpants, Zurik and his paints... She growled under her breath. This needed to be sorted out, and pronto, so that she could get back to Joe in Thistledown Cottage or wherever he was, and explain.

Lizzie tossed on dry clothes and stomped out. "Forget your toiletries, Saffron. Let's start with my interrogation, instead."

"Interrogation?"

"Spill it," Lizzie commanded. "Storm. Fake fiancé. Now."

"Lizzie, I can't." Saffron dropped a plastic pouch full of hair care products and threw herself back onto the bed. "You'll be mad."

"I'm already mad."

"You'll hate me," Saffron whined, hiding behind a curtain of auburn curls.

"I already hate you."

"Do you really?" She sat up, a picture of woe. "I only did it for you."

"Oh, Saff." Lizzie sat down heavily on the foot of the other bed. "This was all just so I could impress Eric Bellamy? I haven't even seen Eric. Meanwhile, no one else is impressed, believe me."

"No, Liz, it wasn't because of Eric." Saffron's usually pale face grew even paler, although there were two spots of color high on her cheeks. "I only came up with that the other day as a cover, because I was desperate."

"You, desperate? I—I don't understand."

Saffron sighed, her expression anxious and distraught, and then she buried her pointy little face in her hands. Lizzie didn't know what to think—this behavior was totally out of character for her unflappable business partner. Nothing ever fazed Saffron. Until now.

"What can it be?" Lizzie prompted, turning over choices like *gambling debts* and *blackmail* in her mind. It all seemed so ridiculous. "What can be this bad?"

"The Velvet Fig," Saffron confessed.

That was out of left field. What did fake fiancés have to do with their business? "Okay. I'll bite. What about it?"

"You were the creative person and I was supposed to be the business half, remember?"

"Of course I remember. Only it didn't work that well because—"

"Because I couldn't find investors," Saffron supplied. She chewed on the tip of a fingernail until it was ragged. "So you came up with a list of potential investors, and I went to see them."

"Right. You went to see the only people we knew with money—Budge and Viv Bellamy, Genevieve Knox and Nana Lambert. And it worked. They all forked over the cash. I know all that," Lizzie stated impatiently. "Cut to the chase."

"I'm getting there." Saffron stood up and started to pace back and forth, waving her hands around, spilling over with excess energy. "Okay, so at first everyone said no. But I was determined. I approached Budge again. But you know Budge—he's a pig. He told me flat out that he didn't think two flighty 'girls' could run a company by themselves."

"So? You should've told him to cram it!"

"There was nowhere else to go! We had to have the start-up capital or there wouldn't be a Velvet Fig. And I knew if I got Budge to sign on, then Viv and the others would, too. All I needed was some silent guy partner. So I told him—'' Saffron threw up her hands ''—I told him your fiancé was also onboard, a real-live *man* with an MBA, who could surely pull our feminine fat out of the fire if we got into trouble.''

Lizzie groaned.

Saffron edged closer. ''It was even easier to lie the next time, when I went to see Genevieve. She was all suspicious and weird and kept quizzing me about you and Eric, like she thought there was some big illicit affair going on and you were going to snatch him out from under her stiff-rumped daughter's nose. It was totally bogus, but I could not convince her.''

''I'm not surprised,'' Lizzie said softly. ''Ever since I've known her, she's been paranoid that someone is going to steal Eric, the world's most eligible bachelor, from Caroline. She'll do anything to keep them together.''

''Including,'' Saffron finished, ''investing in The Velvet Fig. As long as—and only if—you were safely engaged to someone else.''

''Oh, God. This is so sad.'' Lizzie lay back and put her hands over her eyes.

''But it isn't. Sad, I mean. It made them happy, and it didn't change a darn thing about The Velvet Fig. And it was so easy to make up a nice convenient fiancé for you,'' Saffron admitted. ''I mean, it wasn't like we were running into these people every day or anything. And I never said who he was—just that he was smart and handsome and a real asset to The Velvet Fig management team.''

Lizzie choked. "And this MBA paragon was supposed to be *Storm?*"

"It wasn't supposed to be anyone!" Saffron wailed. "Who knew you'd be coming to this stupid wedding with all of them in one place?"

"It doesn't matter now." Lizzie set her jaw. "We have to tell them the truth. Obviously, The Velvet Fig has turned a nice profit and Eric is marrying Caroline. So no one will have a problem with my single status anymore."

"Oh, come on, Lizzie. Grow up." Her face bleak, Saffron twisted a red-gold curl around one finger. "How will they feel when they find out they were bamboozled all this time? They'll pull their money so fast we won't know what hit us. And boom, no more public offering, no more paying back our investors, no more Velvet Fig. Everything we've worked so hard for, down the drain."

Lizzie didn't know what to think.

Saff lifted herself to her knees, and she adopted a beseeching expression. "We were planning to go public with our stock next January. Six lousy months! And we still can. All you have to do is go along with this, for now, for the sake of The Velvet Fig."

Lizzie really, really hated this. If it were just her company, she knew she would cash it in and let the chips fall where they may.

But it was Saffron's company, too, and she couldn't turn her friend out into the cold that easily, not to mention all the other Fig employees who would never find jobs elsewhere. What would happen to Esmie, who needed so much time off to take her sick mom on cruises and bail her wayward daughter out of jail? Or GiGi the receptionist, who was so sweet but couldn't quite say "Fig"? What employer would take a chance on Dick in Accounting, with his résumé full of embezzling charges? Or poor hypochondriac Yvonne who couldn't run the intercom? Or even Oliver the ancient night watchman who had a tendency to fall asleep in midsentence?

To save Saffron, to save all of them, Lizzie knew what she had to do.

She had to keep this farce alive.

Chapter Six

Lizzie kept giving herself pep talks as she dressed for the rehearsal and dinner. Now that she knew the stakes, she would try harder to pull off this fake fiancé scam. Wouldn't she?

It felt terrible to have the two things she prided most—her ability to come through for friends in need and her basic honesty—in conflict this way. Should she go along and lie like a rug? Or should she tell the truth and let her company die, and all of her friends and employees twist in the wind?

It was an impossible choice.

She continued to ponder the options as she slipped into the dress she'd planned for tonight, one of the catalog's coolest items, a long, lean, garnet-red velvet tunic with slits on the sides. The thing that made it stand out was the hand-stenciled design carved right into the fabric on the front panel.

Simple, funky and fun, it was everything she loved about The Velvet Fig. That should've made her feel better about what she was sacrificing on behalf of the company, but it didn't.

Her puffy eyes had settled back to their normal

size, her short hair was easy to finger-comb, and she knew she looked as good as she could. It didn't help.

Listless, she buckled on the matching velvet wedgies, and then poked through one of her boxes for a little beaded purse and a pair of earrings to finish off the outfit. Hmmm... The earrings she wanted weren't there. The purse was, but another just like it in a different color had disappeared. Curious, Lizzie sorted through the rest of the box, concluding that several small items were unaccounted for.

"I suppose Petsy and Viv could've taken them as part of their freebie haul," she said doubtfully. But they hadn't had this box open out there in the parlor.

Could Storm or Zurik have filched them? Or could there really be a thief wandering around the wedding of the millennium, as Winnie had suggested?

Just what she needed—one more thing to worry about. On the other hand, she hadn't thought about Joe or her romantic problems for at least three minutes, and there was something to be said for that.

She exited the parlor bathroom, her new home away from home, to find both Zurik and Storm waiting for her. This had to be the lamest idea ever, but it did cover all the bases. As Saffron had pointed out, if Lizzie sat at dinner between the two men, everybody who thought she was engaged to either of them would be satisfied.

Except Nana, of course, who had it in her head that Lizzie and Joe were the betrothed couple. But there was nothing Lizzie could do about that. After tonight, with the two-fiancé tango, Lizzie didn't expect Joe to ever speak to her again. She steeled her heart against the possibility.

As Zurik and Storm rose from the sofa to greet her, Lizzie decided they were both presentable, if odd in their own individual ways. Storm wore black tie with a dinner jacket, which looked terrific on his pumped-up body, but much too formal for this party, while Zurik was grouchy but clean in a loose white shirt over narrow black trousers.

Zurik still wore his earring, his hair stood up like one of his paintbrushes, and his mouth was twisted into a perpetual scowl. Lizzie was sort of surprised he'd agreed to go along with this at all, but as Saffron had pointed out, he did get a free meal, plus she'd offered him a nice cash bonus if he didn't screw it up. So he was sulky, but up for the scam.

Lizzie glanced between them. Tuxedo Boy on one side, and Cranky Man on the other. Oh, yeah. Walking in with these two wasn't going to raise any eyebrows, was it?

Saffron, spiffy in a pink silk chiffon dress and one of her trademark huge hats, made the trek down to the Folly with them. This was supposed to camouflage the fact that Lizzie had two dates.

"I don't think I can pull this off," Lizzie warned Saffron, as the butterflies in her stomach started to flap their wings and do loop-de-loops. "How am I supposed to eat and pretend and juggle two men at the same time? I don't think it can be done."

Around the big smile she'd pasted on in preparation for their entrance, Saffron replied, "I've had two dates at once before and even *they* didn't know. If I can, you can, because, as we both know, you're a lot smarter than I am. And if all else fails, head for the ladies' room. It's way the heck over on the other side of the lobby, so it'll take you hours to get there and back.''

''I can't face any of these people!''

''You can. You already have.''

''Yes, but then I didn't know what they all thought.''

Storm leaned over his sister. ''What are you two talking about? And what's my motivation for this scene?''

''Your motivation is to act like a human being,'' Lizzie said as kindly as she could manage.

''And to stay away from Viv Bellamy!'' Saffron snapped.

''What are you all bickering about?'' Zurik demanded, sidestepping Lizzie to get in on the conversation. ''Tell me again why I have to be here. I despise these bourgeois mating rituals.''

''You have to be here because we said so,'' Saffron said in a heated tone. ''And because we're paying the bills.''

Zurik lowered his lids and gave her a sultry stare. ''I adore dominating women.''

''Good. Prepare to be dominated.'' But a small, furtive smile played about Saffron's lips, and Lizzie didn't like the looks of it.

She had no time to worry about that, however, since they were almost at the rehearsal at the Folly, and she could already see other guests milling about, apparently waiting for the rest of the bridal party. Surreptitiously, she glanced down at the cheat sheet she'd hidden in the palm of her hand.

Viv plus Petsy: Zurik.

Budge plus Genevieve plus Winnie: Storm.

Nana: Joe.

Joe: ?

She was squinting at it, trying to read the tiny letters.

"Something interesting down there?" inquired a distinctive male voice at her elbow.

Lizzie straightened immediately, rolling her hand into a fist and tucking it behind her back. "Hello, Joe. How are you tonight?"

She gazed wistfully into his devastatingly handsome face, dutifully reminding herself why she had to keep up the fiancé fantasy. *Bummer.* Unlike her two escorts, Joe was dressed just right. In a dark suit and tie, he wasn't flashy or eccentric or anything but perfect.

"Are you okay?" she asked softly. "Your knee wasn't reinjured or anything when you fell into the lake, was it? I was worried about you. And you know, I would be happy to drive you to a hospital if you need to go."

"Not necessary, thanks. I'm just fine." He paused, casting a jaded glance over her two dates. "And you? Decided to travel in a pack tonight, huh?"

"It's safer that way," she replied. Unlike talking to him, which was danger in spades.

"Uh-huh." But he looked very intrigued as she forced herself to walk past him and join the others on their way to the makeshift altar.

After the rehearsal, Genevieve was squalling

about Bianca being late. But thanks to Bianca, Lizzie could study her poem. *This will never work.*

ODETTE was an interesting place, mostly decorated in black and white, with a sleek, classy mood. As Lizzie recalled the story, the name Odette came from a swan in a famous ballet. Even though the hotel's omnipresent swans were worked into the decor, the effect was subtle, and the place was very elegant. The oil paintings on the walls displayed soft-hued ballet dancers in tutus.

Tonight, the tables were covered with fine white linen and decorated with deep mauve roses in silver vases. They were arranged so that there was a long dais across the front, an even longer buffet along the side, and other scattered seating areas around the rectangular room. It looked like some forty people were expected for the rehearsal dinner. Most of them, thank goodness, were people she didn't know.

Lizzie slid into her seat between Storm and Zurik, hunkering down so no one could see her. She noted that the bride and groom and their parents were all lined up at the front table like *The Last Supper.* And not one of them looked happy.

Genevieve and her husband Hainsworth sat on one end, and the chill emanating from the two of them was frigid enough to frighten penguins. Awash in anxiety, Genevieve kept signaling to her waiter for refills on cocktails, and she was popping little pills like there was no tomorrow.

Budge, Rhonda-Wanda-Brenda, and little Fawn took up the opposite end of the table, except Fawn and Lambie were peeking out from under the table and Brenda-Wanda-Rhonda was in a tizzy trying to grab her Fawn out from there, while Budge just ignored both of them.

Viv Bellamy was on the other side of Budge, and she was so bored she was practically snoozing, although she perked up when she saw Storm, calling, "Yoo hoo!" to him and waving her arm.

Wonderful.

As the guests settled in, Budge stood up, removed his cigar for a second, and cleared his throat loudly. "Welcome, friends and relatives and all the rest of you. Tonight's on me, so eat hearty." And then he plunked back into his seat, as people took their signal to head for the elaborate buffet, and waiters circulated with trays of champagne.

Under cover of all that mingling, Lizzie took a long look at the couple in the middle of the head table. She swallowed.

Eric. He was beautiful, there was no other word for it. With his classic, all-American features and polished charm, Eric was one-of-a-kind. If only he weren't glowering like that. It kind of wrecked the picture.

"You'd glower, too, if you were stuck next to Caroline," Lizzie muttered.

The bride-to-be looked almost as puffy as Lizzie had earlier in the day, except this time it really did seem to be the result of tears. Caroline had recently adopted a rather unflattering hairdo, what Lizzie used to call a B-52, a big old helmet head. Under the hard, shellacked hair, Caroline's face was pinched and peeved, and from time to time she turned and sniped at her groom. The words were impossible to make out at this distance, but the general idea was as plain as the B-52 on Caroline's head.

"If those two make it down the aisle, I'm the Queen of Sheba," Lizzie said under her breath.

"Did you say something?" Storm asked. "Nice place, huh? Can't wait to get a fork into that buffet over there. They've got all kinds of cool stuff," he said happily. "You going?"

"Not just yet. But, hey, knock yourself out." Lizzie offered a thin smile that she tried to make more enthusiastic as Genevieve and her assistant passed by. But Gen was a twitchy bundle of nerves and cocktails, and she didn't notice Lizzie or her two fiancés.

So Lizzie found her gaze returning to Eric, as she mused on old times and all the daydreams she'd invested in him.

"Quit mooning over Eric," Saffron whispered from across the table. "You are so obvious."

"I'm not mooning. As a matter of fact..."

As a matter of fact, she had just come to the mind-boggling realization that she no longer had a crush on him. Heavens. When had that happened?

She gave him a good once-over, but there were no weak knees, no topsy-turvy tummy, no sentimental sighs. She just felt sorry for him. Because, boy, did he look like he was having a rotten time.

Storm came gliding back from the buffet with a plate heaped so high he could hardly see around it, and Saffron inquired, "Lizzie, don't you think you should eat something?"

At least she was saved the indignity of picking

out her food in lockstep with her two dates, since they'd already gone and come back while she was having her Eric Epiphany.

The argument at the bride's table picked up volume, and Lizzie chose that moment to sneak up to the buffet, hoping that all of the important people—the ones whose names appeared on her palm—would be otherwise occupied. She had a few shrimp and a strawberry on her plate when she noticed Joe had cut into line right behind her. Her eyes narrowed. Was Joe stalking her, or was it her imagination?

Before she could stop him, he'd covered her hand with his own and flipped it over, intent on reading the notes written on her hand.

"Stop that!"

"You're in luck," he murmured, turning her palm this way and that, trying to get a better angle. "It's all smudged and I can't read it. So, what were you cribbing for? Somebody testing you later tonight?"

"No, it's…" She stalled, trying to come up with a reason to have reference notes written on her hand. "It's etiquette. A few pertinent rules of etiquette. I didn't want to embarrass anyone."

"Ah. You didn't want to embarrass anyone, so you came with two dates?" he asked slyly, reaching over her to nab a roll. He inclined his head back at her table. "Which one are you two-timing?"

What was she supposed to say to that? "It's none of your business" was all she could come up with.

"Lizzie, come on." He angled a hip into the buffet, blocking her path. "You and I both know you're not the type to cheat on the guy you're with. And especially not to rub his face in it. So what gives with this game you're playing?''

Defiantly, she lifted her chin and stared him down. "Maybe I like the variety. I never claimed to be *conventional*," she said, giving the last word a naughty spin.

Joe looked startled, but he recovered quickly. "Are you implying this is a threesome?"

That was exactly what she was implying. But if she'd hoped it would gross him out or make him run away, she was mistaken.

He lifted one dark eyebrow. "Care to make it four?"

She knew he was teasing her—at least she hoped he was teasing her—but that didn't make it any better. "No," she said hotly, abandoning her plate and the buffet and running back to her threesome.

"You shouldn't be talking to him," Saffron complained. "It looks bad."

"I'm not talking to him anymore," Lizzie retorted, just as Budge put a heavy hand on her shoulder. She stiffened.

"Everything all right over here?" he asked heartily. "Everybody having a good time?"

They all smiled politely, all except Zurik, who merely sneered and drank his wine. He muttered something about "wretched excess," but apparently Budge didn't catch it.

"I'm paying for this, so I want everybody to enjoy themselves," Budge hollered. "Chow down. Drink up."

"Oh, we will," Lizzie said with false gaiety.

Clasping her shoulder, Budge bent down to her

ear. "Glad to see you and the boy patched things up. That's what you need, to spend some time together. Hey, Muldoon, some of the younger folks are taking the party to the Cygnet Club after dinner. There'll be a piano player, a little dancing. Maybe you and Storm should try it. Might be just what the love doctor ordered." And then he collared her with one arm and Storm with the other, and practically knocked their heads together.

Lizzie squealed, Storm laughed, and Budge was on his merry way.

"This is downright painful," Lizzie declared, shaking her head to clear the cobwebs.

"But it's working," Saffron reminded her. "Budge bought it, didn't he?"

But not Joe. From all the way across the room, he caught her eye and lazily lifted his wineglass in a salute. She ignored him.

A fresh outburst from Eric and Caroline drew her eyes back to the front. As everyone in the place watched, Eric leapt to his feet, slammed down his napkin and stalked off.

Uh-oh.

In the shocked silence that followed, Caroline burst into tears, her mother rushed to her side, and then Caroline stumbled after Eric, with Genevieve's harried assistant Anne bringing up the rear.

Around the room, clusters of nervous chatter began, and Lizzie half rose, anxious to help.

"Lizzie," Saffron began in an ominous tone, "there's nothing you can do. Besides, Viv Bellamy is on the horizon at four o'clock."

Battle stations. Immediately, Lizzie nudged her

chair away from Storm and looped an arm around Zurik, who said, "Huh? What are you doing?"

She whispered, "You're on call as my boyfriend, remember?"

"Hi, kids!" Viv announced, sailing up with her usual show of energy. She appeared to be the one person in Odette who wasn't worried about the battle raging between the bride and groom. Instead, she beamed at Lizzie and Zurik, and then leaned down and pinched both their cheeks at the same time. "Oh, aren't you two just the cutest couple? I love romance!"

"Thanks, Viv," Lizzie replied, working hard to keep her strained smile from slipping.

Zurik just sneered.

Viv went sailing on. "Listen, Lizzie, you're all set to come for lunch tomorrow at my studio, right? I want to see what you think about putting some of my smaller pieces in your catalog."

They'd already had this discussion, and Lizzie had tried to be diplomatic. "Viv, your work is wonderful, really, but I'm not sure sculptures are right for The Velvet—"

"Yeah, but you won't know till you see, will you?" Viv winked. "I invited Storm to come, too, and you can bring along your fiancé. We'll make it a party."

"I thought I *was* her fiancé," Storm whispered to his sister, as Lizzie kicked him under the table. "Ow. Ow." Apparently Saffron had kicked him from the other side, too.

Blithely unaware, Viv waggled two fingers at Storm. "Don't be a stranger, y'hear? That head table is like death warmed over, especially after that little lover's tiff. I swear, Caroline and Eric are so mopey these days. But what can you do? Young lovers! Always a storm somewhere.'' She hooted with laughter. "Always a storm. Storm, get it?'' As she backed away, Viv called out, "Be sure and come on over, Storm. We'll liven this place up.''

Before he could respond, Saffron told her brother, "No. Absolutely not.''

Storm set his square jaw in a rigid line. "I want to.''

"No.''

"Yes.''

Saffron shook her small fist at Storm. "What's with you, disobeying instructions?''

"This is boring, Saff,'' he protested. "And I like Viv. Plus she wants me to pose for one of her sculptures and I think that could be really good for my career, don't you?''

He looked so unhappy Lizzie began to feel sorry for him. "What does it matter if he has a little fun?'' Lizzie interceded. "Somebody should. Besides, no one's paying attention to us. Who'll care?''

"You people are giving me a headache. Okay, let me think this through.'' Saffron bent over closer to her partner, counting off on her fingers. "Budge already saw you with Storm, and Viv saw you with Zurik. Besides being occupied with the happy couple, Genevieve is so blitzed she won't know if you're dating a Martian.'' She frowned. "Anybody else?''

"Petsy?'' Lizzie's gaze methodically swept the room. "I don't see her. Winnie? She must be help-

ing her mother defuse the war between Eric and
Caro. What about Nana?''

"I think she's safe."

"What about Joe?" Lizzie asked anxiously.
"He's still there, and he's watching me like a
hawk."

Saffron hesitated. "And which one does he think
you're engaged to?"

Lizzie bit her lip, finally admitting, "I think he
knows the truth. He seems to think it's all a big
joke."

"He knows? That's terrible!" Saffron sent Lizzie
an alarmed glance from under the brim of her
droopy hat. "Will he keep his mouth shut?"

"He hasn't said anything yet, but he *is* Budge's
stepson. He may feel a certain loyalty, if he figures
out that Budge's money is involved."

"Oh, no. This is worse than I thought. Better stay
away from him altogether." Rising from their impromptu summit meeting, Saffron announced,
"Okay, Storm, you're clear to go. But not at her
table. Slip a message to one of the waiters and tell
her to meet you outside—and take a hike if you see
Budge, okay?"

"Got it." He was off immediately, cornering a
waiter and scribbling something on a napkin.

"Saff, did you ever consider a career in the
CIA?" Lizzie inquired.

But she didn't answer. "He's doing this all
wrong," Saffron muttered, and she went after her
brother.

Zurik scraped his chair, pushing himself back
from the table. With ill-humor written all over him,

he said, "Hey, if you're done with me, I need to finish that painting by Saturday, remember?"

And then he stalked off, too, grabbing several bottles of wine and a pecan pie off the dessert table on his way out.

Propping her chin in her hands, Lizzie reflected that she'd started this dinner with two dates, and now she had none.

"Don't look now, but one of your fiancés just sneaked out with Viv Bellamy, and the other one is having an intimate encounter with a case of champagne," Joe informed her. Lounging against the wall behind her, he crossed his arms over his chest. "I hate to quote ol' Budge, but you ought to keep a leash on those guys."

"I have to go..." Lizzie stood up abruptly. "I have to go to the ladies' room."

She was out of there so fast it should've made his head spin. Unwilling to look back, Lizzie made a beeline across the gleaming hardwood floor of the lobby, past the huge curving staircase in the corner, not stopping until she was safely inside the powder room.

"Dishonesty is exhausting," she whispered.

"Hi, Lizzie, do you remember me?" A stunning blonde arose from one of the tufted chairs in front of the mirrors. "We met a few times in college. Played tennis, I think."

"Of course, Bianca." Lizzie found a smile for the other bridesmaid, the one who had outraged Genevieve by bringing a mystery baby to the garden party. She hardly knew Bianca, and she remembered being very intimidated by her European sophistication when they were in college. It was hard not to hate a woman that drop-dead gorgeous, but Lizzie still felt sympathy for the beautiful blonde's predicament. "How are you?"

Stupid question. How could she be, when the poor thing had been the center of a maelstrom of controversy ever since she'd arrived?

Lizzie wanted to ask her if the baby was Eric's— that would certainly explain all the brouhaha between the bride and groom, wouldn't it?—but there was no way she was venturing onto that turf. Instead, she hedged her bets with a vague statement like, "The bride and groom seem to be having some trouble, don't they?"

"Yes, they do." Bianca shrugged her slender shoulders. "It's a terrible shame."

"Do you think there's anything we can do? What with all the arguments and tears, I'm starting to wonder whether there's actually going to be a wedding," Lizzie confessed. "We may just be off the hook as bridesmaids."

"Well, you know what they say," Bianca reminded her. "Anything can happen at a Bellamy wedding."

"Oh, right. I've heard that." Given her own recent disasters, Lizzie was thinking of having that little proverb engraved on her forehead.

Bianca excused herself, and Lizzie fooled around with lipstick and a comb, wasting time. Surely everyone had left the rehearsal dinner by now, and she could wander away herself.

What a night. She hadn't partaken of the sumptuous buffet or drunk even a sip of champagne, she'd had to avoid the one person there she liked, and now she had to go back up to her stupid suite and bunk all alone on the sofa!

It was depressing.

But as Lizzie left the ladies' room, she heard the tempting, jazzy strains of a Gershwin tune spilling from the Cygnet Club, the small bar tucked into a corner of the lobby. Budge had mentioned an after-dinner party there, with a piano player and maybe even dancing. This must be it. Lizzie paused a moment next to a potted palm, listening. She couldn't quite catch the singer's words, but the piano was coming across loud and clear.

"Fascinating Rhythm," she thought, melting under the spell of the music. She loved Gershwin.

What could it hurt to take a peek? Just for a second, she wanted to enjoy the music and the moment, maybe even block out her troubles. She felt better just thinking about it.

And hadn't Budge said this was a party for the younger folks, not the stuffy types she'd been attempting to impress all night? So it ought to be perfectly safe to slip into the shadows and listen to the piano. No fuss, no muss, no fiancés.

She began to hum along with the song as she ducked in the door to the dark, woody, intimate Cygnet Club.

Lizzie stopped in her tracks. Joe was there. It was as if his physical presence reached out and smacked her on the head, even when he wasn't that near. On a stool at the bar, he was turned away from her, and he appeared to be nursing a beer.

"If I want to listen to the music, I'm not letting

him run me off," she murmured defiantly. "Besides, he doesn't even know I'm here."

Determined to enjoy herself, Lizzie eased further into the bar, taking up a position behind a pillar, where she was completely blocked from Joe, but could still see the piano and the dance floor.

And what was that about a dance party for the young folks? The only dancer out there at the moment was dear old Nana, kicking up her heels on the hardwood floor, doing something that looked like the Charleston mixed with the Funky Chicken.

"At least someone is enjoying herself," Lizzie said aloud, and her lips curved into a crooked smile. There was no way to avoid a good mood while watching Nana get down and dirty.

Switching from "Fascinating Rhythm" to "I Got Rhythm," the pianist picked up his pace, his fingers flying over the keys. Eager to keep up, Nana put her dance into overdrive, swinging out with a vintage-looking, beaded purse that dangled from her wrist. Everyone else steered clear of the dance floor, sensing danger from the flying object.

Lizzie tipped her head to one side, keeping an eye on the purse as it flipped and flapped in a wild figure eight. It looked awfully familiar. In fact, she now realized it was the very one that was missing from The Velvet Fig collection.

"Gee, maybe I've found our cat burglar," Lizzie said under her breath. Now wouldn't that be interesting? And complicated.

Because if the thief *was* Nana, what could she do? She was hardly going to turn the sweet old lady over to the cops, or even unmask her to her nearest and dearest as a kleptomaniac. What with a battling bride and groom, a mother of the bride who was headed for a breakdown, one bridesmaid with a psychotic four-year-old and another with an unidentified baby, there was just no room at this wedding for a klepto grandmother.

But she couldn't just sit back and let Nana lift things right and left, either. Much better to handle it herself, to nip Nana's career as a petty thief in the bud with no one the wiser.

First, I really have to make sure I'm right about that purse, Lizzie decided. She scooted a little closer so she could get a better look.

But the piano player chose a slower song—"Let's face the Music and Dance," with lyrics about there being trouble ahead and paying the piper, which Lizzie didn't need to hear.

Reacting to the change in tempo, Nana grabbed a Kevin off a bar stool and started to fox-trot, which hid the evening bag from Lizzie's view.

So what now? There was no other way.

"I have to get onto that dance floor," Lizzie said grimly. If she could just get waltzed around, right up next to Nana, she was sure she could surreptitiously check out the evening bag. "Maybe I can even steal it back."

But first things first. She needed a dancing partner.

She chewed her lip, casting a speculative glance around the Cygnet Club. "If I go out there onto the floor, Joe is going to see me, anyway, so I might as well come right out and ask him to be the one. Okay, so he has a bum knee. It's a slow one. He'll be fine.''

That sounded plausible, didn't it? And if the side effect of this skulduggery was that she got to dance with Joe, well, hey, it was all for a good cause.

"Excuse me," she ventured softly, sliding onto a stool next to him. "Can I talk to you for a minute?"

He turned her way. His gaze was wary, and Lizzie felt herself flushing under his scrutiny.

Finally, he spoke. "I thought you were avoiding me. You know, running to the rest room, hiding behind pillars, that sort of thing."

So he'd seen her. She should've known he would pick up her scent. Didn't she know when *he* was there, even without a word, without a look?

"I wasn't avoiding you. Not exactly," she hedged. "And besides, this is something different. I need your help."

"Well, hallelujah." Joe spun around all the way. "You've decided to come clean on whatever scam you and Saffron are running, and you want me to help you out of the jam. Whatever I can do, Lizzie. Fire away."

"No. I mean, this has nothing to do with you and me, or me and Storm, or me and Zurik. None of that," she said hastily. "This is a rescue mission."

"Uh-huh."

"I mean," Lizzie continued, feeling herself sink into deeper and deeper water, "I figured you were the only other person here who had a social conscience. And liked saving people. Besides me, I mean."

"Did you ever consider rescuing yourself first?" he asked, with more than a hint of irony.

"I don't need to be rescued."

"Uh-huh," he repeated, in that same infuriating tone. Then he just looked at her, took a swallow of beer, and let her hang there. His sexy lips pressed into a narrow line, and his eyes looked hard and judgmental, like glittering green glass.

"So?" Lizzie prompted. "You want to help or not?"

Under his breath, Joe muttered, "I must be nuts." But then he added, "Who is it we're saving? And from what?"

"Okay, here's the plan." Quickly, Lizzie filled him in on the cat burglar rumors, the missing items from her stock, and the purse Nana was flashing around. "So I'm pretty sure it's her. The thief, I mean. And all you have to do," she concluded, "is dance me over to her, and then, oh, I don't know, dip me or something, just long enough for me to get a good look. And then if it *is* The Velvet Fig purse, we have to figure out some way to steal it back. Plus whatever other booty she's got. Quietly."

"Uh-huh."

Lizzie sank down on her stool. "Will you stop saying that? Do you want to dance with me or not?"

Joe stood, pushing away from the bar. "I thought you'd never ask."

"One last thing."

"What now?"

Lizzie didn't know how to put this. "You can

dance, can't you? It won't hurt your leg or any-thing?''

He smiled. "I think I can manage."

And then he held out his hand.

Chapter Seven

With a deep breath, Lizzie took his hand.

As he swung her into his embrace, his arms felt warm and strong around her, and Lizzie wondered just how far over her head this dance might get.

She tried to keep things light, but it wasn't easy. "How in the world do you know how to dance?" she asked, as she concentrated on matching her steps to his. "It's not the image I would've picked for you. Who ever heard of a macho Chicago firefighter who can do the two-step?"

"Fireman's Ball."

"Are you serious?" Lizzie laughed. "You're not serious."

"Sure I am. I'm off my game, of course, with this stupid knee, but I can still stumble along." He shrugged, tightening his arm around her waist, nudging her closer.

Whoa. This wasn't a dance, it was a straitjacket. Lizzie felt breathless and a little hot, and her heartbeat accelerated. But she closed her eyes, letting herself snuggle closer for just a second. A second couldn't hurt, could it? She'd get back to her goal sooner or later, and in the meantime...

In the meantime, this felt so right, she must have been born to dance in Joe Bellamy's arms.

Now the diabolical pianist had struck up "Embraceable You," and the man was singing, in a soft, achingly romantic voice, about just how much he wanted to put his arms around the woman he loved.

Even without Joe so very near, the song would've made Lizzie swoon. Was this a conspiracy?

She remembered what Nana Lambert had said about her beloved matador. *When we tangoed, I thought the world would end.* This was no tango, and neither of them would ever be mistaken for Fred or Ginger, but Lizzie still understood the sentiment. There was something to be said for dim lights, soft music and someone to hold you tight.

Her knees felt like warm butter, and she was clumsier than she should've been. "This is very nice," she whispered.

"You know, Lizzie, I didn't get a chance to tell you, but you look beautiful tonight."

Joe spoke the words in such a sweet, simple tone that Lizzie felt warm and fuzzy from the inside out. Nobody ever told her that she was beautiful. People told her she was smart all the time. Funny almost as often, crazy even. But beautiful? Never.

"You look really pretty in red," he murmured into her ear. "And your dress is as soft as you are."

"It's from my store. The Velvet Fig."

"Mmm..."

It wasn't even a word, but it spoke volumes about

what he thought about her dress and how she felt there in his embrace. She loved it.

She was so hypnotized by the whole experience she almost forgot what she was doing there on the dance floor. But Nana had ditched her Kevin, preferring a free-form interpretive dance solo, with the swinging evening bag as a prop. When it bopped Lizzie right in the bottom, she had no choice but to get back to business. *Oh, yeah.* One purple beaded bag that didn't belong to Nana Lambert.

"Joe, I'm sorry to break this up." *Sorrier than you'll ever know.* "But we're supposed to be on a mission—the stolen purse, remember?"

Joe's mouth curved into a dark smile, but he gamely guided Lizzie that way. "Did you say you wanted to dip?"

"Well, yes, but I don't think we actually have to—"

Too late. One minute she was secure in the circle of his arms, the next she was dangling in space, upside down, with Nana's purse inches from her nose.

Joe reeled her back in, and Lizzie said sadly, "I just made a positive ID. It's one of mine."

"So, should we frisk her? Beat her with a rubber hose?" His tone was well past sardonic. "This is your mission, Lizzie. What do you want to do next?"

I want to keep dancing with you till the cows come home. If only that darn "Embraceable" song would stop. Lizzie focused. "I guess we corner her and tell her we know she stole it and demand that she stop."

"And how do we corner her?" Joe's gaze swept over Nana, who was still experiencing boogie-woogie fever. "Looks like we'll have to get a big hook and drag her off. What is she doing?"

"Modern dance à la Isadora." When he looked blank, Lizzie continued, "I guess you never heard the whole story. Nana is convinced she's the reincarnation of Isadora Duncan. You know, the dancer?"

"Huh?"

"I know—it sounds crazy. But until this klepto-mania thing, she was otherwise harmless, so nobody ever worried about it too much." Lizzie smiled. "Shirley MacLaine thinks she's reincarnated from Cleopatra, and Nana Lambert thinks she's the second coming of Isadora Duncan. Of course, it's complicated by the fact that Nana was born ten years before Isadora Duncan died, so even people who believe in reincarnation don't get her theory. But there's no way to convince her, and she's been just sure about this for ages, so what can you do? But that's why she likes to dance so much."

"Because her inner Isadora is coming out?"

"Exactly."

She could tell Joe was working hard not to laugh out loud. Or choke or something. He kept glancing at Nana and then back at Lizzie, as if trying to decide whether she was pulling his leg. "Okay," he said finally. "As long as she's having fun."

"It's true, I swear." Lizzie crossed her heart with one finger, thinking once again what a great guy he was. Most men would tell her it was stupid and that

Nana Lambert should be locked up. Joe just shrugged. *As long as she's having fun.*

"Why don't I take Nana for a spin?" Joe suggested. "I have a feeling she'll lead, but I might be able to maneuver her out the door."

"Great idea." So why did Lizzie feel so bereft the minute his hand slipped away from her back, leaving her there alone on the dance floor, as he crossed to pick up Nana?

"Hello, Nana. Do you remember me?" he asked, carefully enunciating every word.

"Of course, dear. You're the matador!"

"That's right. How about another tango?" He offered his hand, and the diminutive old lady giggled girlishly.

"I do so love to tango." Slipping her delicate hand into his, she whispered loudly, "This isn't really tango music, dear, but we can improvise. I'm good at it."

"So am I," Joe said. He winked at Lizzie over Nana's silver pin curls. "So am I."

As the music swelled into "Puttin' on the Ritz" or something equally inappropriate, Joe and Nana did a halting tango toward the door. Nana's wrinkled face was set with concentration as she lifted her tiny slippers in intricate steps that bore no relation to anything Joe did. Lizzie could tell Nana was fighting him on the direction they took, but Joe was stronger.

Lizzie scrambled behind them, unwilling to let her opportunity get away from her. And when Joe swirled Nana out the door of the Cygnet Club, giving her a final twirl, Lizzie was right there to pick up the pieces. Or the purse, anyway.

"Oh, my, I seem to have dropped my bag," Nana said sweetly.

Lizzie was all sympathy as she pointed out, "Nana, that's my bag. You took it by mistake."

"Oh, dear, no. I don't eat steak," Nana responded innocently. "I swore off red meat back in '37."

Lizzie was stuck after that one. "Joe? Can you help me out here?"

"How can I help? She thinks I'm a matador."

"What, dear?" Nana's bright eyes sparkled as she gazed from face to the other. "Are you worried about something?"

"Stealing," Lizzie practically shouted. "This purse is *stolen*."

"It is?" Nana's eyes were as round as saucers. "I'm so glad I took it, then. I wouldn't want to know I left it with a thief! This door upstairs was open, and I walked right in, and there were all these pretty things, in just my favorite shade of lilac. I knew they were meant for me."

"Nana," Lizzie said severely. "You mustn't take any more things. I don't mind if you keep the purse—*you can keep the purse*—but *no more*. Promise?"

Nana blinked. "I felt so sure it was meant for me."

"Oh, boy." Lizzie was just about ready to throw in the towel. "Keep the purse, okay?" She handed it back and patted the old lady's hand. To Joe, she added, "We'll just tell everyone to be sure and lock their doors."

As Nana toddled back to the bar to get a few more

dances in, Joe took Lizzie's arm. "I thought we were supposed to rescue her from her life of crime."

"I tried," Lizzie insisted. "What more could I do? If Nana gets carted off in handcuffs for picking Budge's pocket, I will feel terrible, but what could I do?"

Dryly, he asked, "So there *does* come a point at which you decide one of your harebrained rescue schemes isn't working and you should give it up?"

Lizzie stopped. She knew where this was going. Storm, Zurik, Saffron, yadda, yadda, yadda. "Aw, jeez. Are we back on that again?"

"You really think I'm going to give up?"

She made a face at him. "So there *doesn't* come a point at which you decide your rescue scheme isn't working and you should give it up?"

Joe stuck his hands in his pockets and gazed down at her, his green eyes steady and unconcerned. "Nope."

She didn't know whether to kiss him or smack him. Or even worse, spill her guts. Now that they'd kissed and danced and plotted together, she really, really wanted to confide in him, to clear the air and restore his good opinion of her. But how would telling the truth do that?

Joe had already told her he hated pretense and liars, and this fiancé thing was chock full of both.

He was also related to Budge, her major investor, the very one who had been lied to from the beginning, who might, in fact, be able to charge them all with fraud and throw them in the pokey if the real story came out. Wouldn't Joe feel obligated to tell Budge, his stepfather, the truth?

And speaking of Budge... "What a mess," Lizzie muttered.

Here she was, standing in the lobby with Joe, all intertwined and cozy. If Budge caught a whiff of this, after already witnessing the clinch at the swan pond, her goose was cooked.

"Lizzie," Joe prompted, in a husky, beguiling tone. He trailed a finger over the curve of her cheek. "You know you want to tell me."

Aw, jeez. "I do. I wish—"

She was saved from finishing that sentence when cries of alarm dwarfed the music coming from inside the Cygnet Club.

Joe's ears seemed to perk up. "What was that?"

As they leaned in the door to see what the matter was, both spotted Nana Lambert, now dancing *on* the bar. The piano player stopped in midnote, small clusters of guests froze where they sat, but it didn't interfere with Nana's version of Riverdance to music only she could hear. Her dainty dancing slippers veered closer to the edge of the bar with every tip-tap.

And once again, it was Joe who ran to the rescue.

He turned back at the last moment, dropping a kiss on Lizzie's cheek. "I've got to get her down from there before she hurts herself."

"I know. If you don't, I will."

"I know." He grinned, wagging a finger at her. "But don't think this is over. I'm not giving up on you."

She couldn't decide if that was the good news or the bad news. But she stayed there, clinging to the door, watching as Joe scooped up the frail little lady in his strong arms and swung her down to safety. The Cygnet Club patrons cheered, and Nana threw her arms around him, puckered up and smooched him on the lips. Then she resurrected her buck-and-wing without even missing a beat.

Lizzie smiled. What a guy.

"Excuse me," someone said gloomily behind her.

Stunned, Lizzie whirled. Eric? She would've known that voice anywhere. It was the voice she'd heard in her dreams ever since freshman year in college.

Without acknowledging her, Eric entered the Cygnet Club, walked straight to a table in the back corner, and ordered a stiff drink.

Wow. This wasn't like him at all. All by himself, drinking, looking like he'd been hit by a truck?

Glad to have an excuse to put the confusing pas de deux with Joe behind her, Lizzie hightailed it over to comfort Eric in his hour of need.

So what if her first rescue mission of the night had fizzled? That only gave her more incentive to make this one work.

EVERYBODY IN THE BAR was treating him like a hero. Everybody except Lizzie. As Joe turned down yet another offer of a free drink, he frowned, watching her back there in the corner with his stepbrother, Eric the Perfect.

Their heads were close together, while Lizzie whispered soothing words into a morose Eric's ear. Joe would've given his good leg to know exactly what counsel she was offering.

Was she trying to save Eric's shaky wedding, so

obviously hanging by a thread? Or was she trying to make *sure* it got called off?

Eric, whatever you do, you have to walk down that aisle?

Or, *Eric, you deserve better. Dump the witch and run away with me?*

It was no secret that Lizzie'd had an old crush on the groom. But was it still alive? And what—if anything—did that have to do with all this nutty fiancé business?

Confused and almost as gloomy as his stepbrother, Joe sat back down on his bar stool and decided to wait her out. When she was ready to leave, he'd insist on walking her up to her room. At least that way he could make sure he wasn't meeting Eric. And surely then he could get some answers out of her.

So there he sat, nursing the same beer, growing less and less happy as Eric clasped her hands in his, as she poured sympathy on the poor misunderstood groom, as the piano player kept tinkling catchy, romantic tunes that sounded like Lizzie.

Joe eased the kinks out of his injured leg. "I actually danced with her," he muttered, "threatening life and limb. And what happens? The minute my back is turned, she runs off with Eric!" He would've growled if it wouldn't have scared half the patrons at the Cygnet Club.

Finally, Eric and Lizzie rose from their booth and wandered over to the exit. With an arm casually draped around Lizzie's shoulders, Eric bent and kissed her on the cheek, right there in the doorway, where half the wedding guests could see. And then he walked off into the lobby, none the worse for wear, as his stepbrother silently fumed behind him.

Hands on her hips, Lizzie slapped her velvet wedgies on the hardwood floor as she marched right over to Joe.

"Well?" she demanded. "Did you really think I wouldn't notice you sitting here, spying on me?"

"Did you really think the entire universe wouldn't notice you back in the corner necking with the groom?"

"Necking with the...?" Lizzie's dark blue eyes sparkled with anger. "I was just trying to help and you know it!"

"Lizzie, you're always just trying to help. And you get into more trouble than any ten women I know."

"So why are you waiting around for me?" she snapped.

Joe rose. "I'm walking you to your room. Yeah, I know. I need my head examined. But you intrigue me, because I'll be damned if I can figure you out."

Lizzie defrosted a little as they waited for the antique brass elevator, a little more as it lurched upstairs. She still hadn't told him anything he wanted to hear, but she was actually smiling as she slid open the door to the Prince Siegfried Suite.

Striding into the parlor, Lizzie asked, "Didn't you think it was really funny when Nana started everyone doing the Macarena—"

But then she broke off abruptly.

There was Storm, the muscle man, wearing nothing but a pair of skintight briefs, sprawled on the couch watching TV. Over in the chair, the oddball painter was also bare-chested. The bottom half of him was hidden under a room service cart, off which he was eating a huge, sloppy ice-cream sundae. And his hair—which looked as if it didn't know the meaning of the word *comb*—now appeared to have been smeared with part of his sundae instead of mousse.

"Hi," both men offered.

"Don't stand up!" she said hastily. Her face had taken on a rosy pink glow.

"What was it you called this little arrangement, Lizzie?" Joe had already cut her more slack than any woman he knew. This was too much, even for him. "Unconventional? Isn't that what you said? That's an understatement."

"Joe, I—"

But he was out of there. Whatever was going on in the Prince Siegfried Suite, Joe didn't want to know.

Friday: You're invited to a Bachelor Bash!

LIZZIE WOKE UP LATE, stiff and cranky on her uncomfortable sofa bed. She almost turned over and went back to sleep, but she knew she'd have nightmares. On the other hand, no nightmare could compete with her waking life at this moment.

Still, she got up, wrapped herself in the sheet just in case any of her idiotic roommates happened to traipse through the parlor, and tried to find a shower without a body already in it.

Three bathrooms in this place, and they were all taken! She wanted to scream.

But angry as she was at her selfish, impossible suitemates, all she could think about was the look on Joe's face when he saw Storm and Zurik *both* making themselves at home in her suite.

If it weren't so tragic, it would be funny. Lizzie wasn't laughing.

"I don't know why you're so crabby," Saffron declared, perching on the sofa long enough to lace up her narrow granny boots.

"Maybe it's sleep deprivation," Lizzie groused.

Saffron pursed her lips. "You shouldn't have brought him up here in the first place. You were supposed to be staying away from him."

"It never occurred to me that those two morons would be hanging around at midnight half-naked. They have bedrooms. Why weren't they in them?" Lizzie swept up her sheet with a grand flourish and collected her toothbrush and shampoo. "Besides, Storm got to go off with Viv, and Zurik got to come back to his painting, which is his true love. Why am I the only one who doesn't get to have any fun?"

Saffron rolled her eyes. "Because you're the president of The Velvet Fig, and if you get caught having fun with the wrong guy, there won't *be* a Velvet Fig."

Lizzie was so irritated she didn't even respond. Head held high, she went into the kitchen and made herself a cup of tea. She didn't speak to anyone, waiting patiently until both Saffron and Storm had left the suite, and Zurik was securely latched in with his paints.

She took her time in the bathtub, rinsing, dawdling, finally slipping into a simple, sky-blue tank dress made of sueded silk that felt terrific next to her skin. Her hair wasn't cooperating, but she was only headed to lunch with Viv after all, so she squashed on a wide-brimmed, purple straw hat that covered most of it.

How odd to feel so thrilled by the prospect of a meeting with Viv Bellamy, just so she could get away from Swan's Folly and all these annoying people. She'd originally thought that Viv's lunch plans—and the crazy idea to sell some of her lurid sculptures in their catalog—were a major waste of time.

But now she was actually looking forward to it. At least this was business, and Lizzie felt competent to handle that.

Unlike her personal life.

Of course, it was going to be tricky to turn down Viv's artwork, but Lizzie told herself she was just going to have to be tactful. Given that Viv was an investor, and a major one at that, Lizzie didn't want to come right out and tell her what a terrible idea it was to put cold, hard statues in a catalog full of lush, plush clothes and accessories for the touchable woman. Sculptures of naked men—even small ones—just didn't fit.

As Lizzie put the finishing touches on her outfit, she said out loud, "You know, Viv, I like you. I appreciate the outlandish, funny side of you, and I think you're a hoot to have around. God knows I like you better than any of my other investors. But you can also be a real pain when the mood strikes you."

The words *arrogant* and *demanding* came to mind.

So Lizzie knew she had to toe a fine line with Viv—be charming, discreet and supportive, and say absolutely nothing that could lead Viv to find out that the women of The Velvet Fig had been pulling the wool over her eyes for years.

"God forbid," Lizzie shuddered, hoping to avoid a showdown with loud, violent, crazy Viv as long as she lived. If she'd been wearing boots instead of sandals, she would've been shaking in them.

The last thing Lizzie wanted to do was face another day at Swan's Folly, but she took a deep breath and hurried out of the Prince Siegfried Suite. After a quick spin down the massive, curving mahogany stairs, Lizzie hailed Viv, who was already waiting next to a potted palm on the other side of the front desk.

Uh-oh. Saffron was there, too, standing next to Viv like the cat that ate the canary.

"I didn't expect you to join us," Lizzie said with a definite chill.

Saffron smiled, her usual saucy grin. For a small woman, she was quite curvy, and she looked more voluptuous than usual in a leopard-print knit dress with a deep neckline. Saffron only dressed like that when there was a man she wanted to impress. Lizzie narrowed her eyes. Who was the target?

"Viv asked me to come along," Saffron explained. "I didn't want to miss seeing her fabulous sculptures, did I? Plus, Viv, your weekend studio— a houseboat, isn't it?—sounds so interesting I just have to see it for myself."

Viv chuckled and squeezed Saffron, almost knocking off the vintage 1920s cloche she was wearing pulled down to her eyebrows.

As they chatted about Viv's country house, Lizzie decided she had better get rid of the chip on her shoulder. After all, there was no reason Saffron shouldn't come along, and it might make things easier. The more the merrier, right? She looked around. "So, are we ready? Are we taking your car, Viv?"

"We can't leave without the others," Viv informed her.

"Others?" Lizzie echoed. "What others?"

"The men, hon." Viv laughed. "What fun is it without any men around?" Gazing past Lizzie, she called out, "Here we are—over here."

As she turned, Lizzie's mouth dropped open. Zurik?

Viv caught the surly painter and told him how happy she was he was coming, too, while Saffron whispered, "She told me in no uncertain terms to be sure to bring your fiancé. This is the one she thinks is him, right?"

"I don't know," Lizzie retorted. "I washed the secret code off my hand last night."

"Lizzie, I think your fiancé and I have so much to share in the world of art. Don't we, hon?"

Okay, so Viv definitely had Zurik pegged as the *fiancé du jour.*

And then Storm showed up, just to keep things interesting.

"I twisted Storm's arm," Viv told the others. "Didn't I, cutie-pie?" She poked him in the ribs, making him blush and giggle. "I am dying for

Storm to pose for me. So he definitely needs to see my work, don't you think? Oh, this is going to be such a fun party!''

"I'm having fun already," Lizzie said grimly.

But the surprises weren't over. Just as she thought this lunch couldn't get any more uncomfortable, Viv announced that the last guest had arrived, and they were ready to go.

Last guest? Lizzie glanced over her shoulder. She swore under her breath. Not Joe, too!

"I haven't spent any real time with my favorite stepson in years!" Viv told the others as she made little smacking noises at Joe. "Best thing Budge ever did was bring you into the fold, sweetie."

Lovely.

And so the six of them all piled into the limo Viv had brought around to drive them to her combination houseboat-studio-weekend retreat. As soon as the door closed, Viv started cooing at Storm and Zurik started whining to a surprisingly attentive Saffron about his trials as an *artiste*.

Joe was jammed up against Lizzie, his long legs brushing the silk of her dress. He didn't say anything, but he sent her more than a few mocking looks, as if he knew exactly what was going on and could blow her ruse sky-high any second. She supposed this smug attitude was better than last night, when he was mad at her. But maybe not.

She tried to talk to Zurik, really she did, because she could see that Viv was wondering what was up with the two of them. But he was creepy!

Although Saffron didn't seem to think so. She was pressing her curves into him like crazy, and he wasn't exactly backing off. So, when Viv wasn't drooling on Storm, she was looking at Lizzie with pity brimming in her eyes.

Lizzie knew that look. It said, *Your boyfriend is betraying you with your partner and you're too stupid to notice. Poor Lizzie.*

Poor Lizzie, indeed!

She had never been so happy to tumble out of a car as she was to get out of that limo. They pulled up to Viv's adorable houseboat, made the appropriate oohs and aahs, and filed in for lunch.

"I had it specially built," Viv explained, as she led them to the back deck where their luncheon was being served. "It's called the *Vivacious.* Viv-*Vivacious,* get it? Three stories, and the top one— my studio—has extrahigh ceilings so I can fit my biggest sculptures. Isn't that great?"

Great. Viv had set up a round table on the deck, where mild summer breezes blew in off Geneva Lake. It was a lovely spot, and Lizzie knew she would've enjoyed it under other circumstances. But not these. Trust Viv to seat them boy-girl-boy-girl, which put Lizzie between Zurik, her supposed fiancé for today, and Joe.

Under his thumb. Right where she didn't want to be.

"Storm, I just can't wait to get you out of that shirt and carved in stone," Viv said admiringly, paying no attention to the food as the caterer set plates of lobster salad in front of them.

A growing boy, Storm tucked in right away, but he basked in the admiration of his newfound friend.

Over on the other side, Saffron and Zurik were

whispering to each other, sharing some sort of private joke.

Joe didn't say anything, just watched her. So Lizzie folded and refolded her napkin, ignoring everyone.

"Liz, honey, you're awfully quiet," Viv said, glaring at Saffron and Zurik, who had been giggling just a second ago.

"Oh, I'm fine," Lizzie replied quickly. "I was just a bit unprepared, for a social occasion, I mean. I thought this was a business lunch."

"It will be later, hon. Plenty of time for that." A fleeting look of worry crossed Mrs. Bellamy's brow. "I thought you could use the relaxation, to tell you the truth, and I hoped you and your beau might enjoy some time together. I think my little home away from home here is pretty romantic, don't you?"

"Yes, definitely." Lizzie found a smile. "I was just expecting—"

"Sometimes you have to roll with the punches, hon," Viv advised. Lizzie knew the older woman was trying to be kind, to telegraph warnings about Saffron and Zurik, and she felt massive guilt that it was all a sham. "And, Liz, I didn't mean to bring this up, but it's probably better to lay our cards on the table."

Lizzie gulped. "I don't think—"

"No, no, let me have my say. I talked to Genevieve Knox this morning, and she says you and my son—Eric, I mean—were getting pretty chummy last night. Now I know Gen is as paranoid as they come, but if you and your boyfriend there are having any trouble—you know, you run after Eric so now he does payback with your friend—and this is all because you're still carrying a torch for my son, well—'' Viv fanned herself with her napkin ''—I'd feel just awful.''

Lizzie knew her face must be the same color as the strawberry tart by now. ''No,'' she said finally, when she could get a word in edgewise. ''There's no problem. Everything is fine. Dandy. A-okay. Right, *darling?*'' With a tight smile, Lizzie picked up Zurik's hand and squeezed it, hard enough to keep him from painting for a few hours at least.

''If you say so.'' But disbelief was written all over Viv Bellamy.

Nobody else knew what to say, so everyone talked at once. Everyone but Joe, who sat back and observed all the machinations being played out in front of him. Lizzie could swear she detected a spark of mischief in his eyes that threatened to turn into an all-out blaze.

He was enjoying this! She was sure of it. The man was beyond annoying.

She had never eaten lunch so fast in her life, but she was dying to be away from that table. ''Viv,'' Lizzie said brightly, ''let's see that sculpture. Time's a-wastin'.''

Still entwined around one of Storm's enormous biceps, Mrs. Bellamy led them up into the second floor of her houseboat, where she had an expansive, pure white studio. There was a little plaster dust, but otherwise, just the sculptures themselves—one huge one, about eight feet tall, and several smaller pieces. But they were all men, quite naked men, and with very impressive...

Even mentally, Lizzie couldn't go there. *Equipment,* she finished for herself. *Impressive equipment.*

Lizzie was still feeling light-headed from the impact of all that male pulchritude, when Viv made a major boo-boo. Puffed up with pride, she asked Zurik what he thought of her artwork.

"You call this art?" he asked with a sniff. "I've seen better from third graders." He looked down his nose at one gigantic example of Viv's fascination with the phallus. "Disgraceful. It's not even close to scale."

Saffron laughed. "He's joking, of course."

"Of course!" Lizzie chorused. "What a kidder!"

But Viv's face was practically purple. "Lizzie, may I speak to you in private?"

Feeling as if she were headed for the principal's office, Lizzie dutifully let herself be led around to the other side of the biggest sculpture.

With him and his "equipment" looming up there, Viv lowered her voice. "Okay, I am going to say this for your own good," she began. "You need to dump that jerk. He's cheating on you, he's rude, and he has lousy taste in art. Find a nice, sweet boy like Storm. Or Joe."

"That's okay…"

But Viv was not to be denied. With one hand on the statue's colossal plaster thigh, Viv poked her head around and called out, "Joe? Joe, honey? You aren't dating anyone, are you?"

Lizzie wondered what it would cost to hire someone to kill her and put her out of her misery, right then and there.

Chapter Eight

Viv was trying to match him up with Lizzie. Now
there was a dandy idea. Joe laughed it off, enjoying
the dark humor in Viv's suggestion.

But as he guffawed, Lizzie's face turned as red
as a beet. Mumbling something about artwork and
her catalog, she made a show of turning away from
all of them, carefully examining the smaller sculptures head to toe. He could see the rigid line of her
back and neck, and he could tell she was holding
herself together only with supreme effort.

Joe began to feel about two inches tall himself.
He wasn't a mean person. Really. Okay, so he'd
enjoyed watching Lizzie squirm in the limo, and
even at lunch. With the games she was playing, she
deserved to squirm.

But no one deserved this sort of humiliation.

Having had her say, Viv was back vamping
Storm, and Saffron appeared to be lecturing that horrible painter guy on the finer points of lunch guest
etiquette. But Lizzie lingered back behind the towering plaster he-man, unwilling to come out.

With a sigh, Joe went to go get her. Looked like

it had to be Joe Bellamy, everybody's hero, to the rescue one more time.

"Don't even talk to me," she said tersely.

Joe stuck a hand in his pocket. "You don't know what I'm going to say."

Lizzie sent him a quick glance. "Don't say anything. Just keep laughing. I love being the butt of your jokes."

He sat on the base of the statue, stretching out his leg, wincing as he bent his knee. "Okay, so I'm sorry I laughed. But you have to admit, it's pretty funny—Viv playing matchmaker while your suite is already stuffed to the gills with men."

Shaking her head, Lizzie said hotly, "You have to know—"

"What I know is that you are hip-deep in doo-doo, and I'm willing to bet your pal Saffron is the one who got you there. I'm right, aren't I?"

Lizzie's eyes widened. *Got it in one.* Joe regarded her dryly, not giving an inch. If she was this miserable, maybe it was time for some home truths. Maybe it was time for an intervention. He'd done it for a friend with an alcohol problem, and a colleague hooked on painkillers. So maybe Lizzie was addicted to being walked on—maybe she needed a Doormat Intervention.

"I think," he said calmly, "that you are being taken advantage of by just about everyone you know, with Saffron at the top of the list."

Muttering under her breath, Lizzie spun away from him in a twirl of sky-blue silk.

But he wasn't finished with her yet. Joe pulled her back to face him, tugging on her hand, dragging her right up against his good leg. "If I were you, I would rethink my friendship with that nitwit."

"How dare you tell me who I can and cannot be friends with?" she stormed.

He ignored it. "And if I were you, I would take a hard look at my life in general."

"Because you don't like one of my friends?" She rolled her eyes. "Gee, thanks, Dad. Sorry I'm hanging out with the wrong crowd."

"Has anyone ever told you that you might be, well, an enabler?" he asked, trying to keep his tone gentle. "You really might want to consider talking to someone. I have a cousin who's a shrink if you're interested."

"An enabler? A shrink?" she cried. "I have never been so insulted in my life!"

"Aren't you the one who thinks everyone from Budge to Lambie would benefit from therapy?" he reminded her.

"Well, maybe. But that's different!"

He refrained from saying anything about geese and ganders or pots and kettles. "Lizzie," Joe soothed, "in your heart, you know I'm right. You know I'm only suggesting this for your own good."

"My own good?" That seemed to infuriate her even further, and she snatched her hand away from him. "I'm the one who does the rescuing around here, thank you very much, and I don't need you— or Viv, or anyone else—interfering in my life or trying to tell me what's for my own good. God, I hate that!"

So the world's biggest meddler didn't like being meddled with herself. Surprise, surprise.

She raised a hand, cutting off whatever objection he planned to make. "Okay, so I admit things are a bit confused at the moment. But I can handle it. I can sort it out."

"Confused?" Joe ran a hasty hand through his hair. "That's what you call having two different fiancés, both of them staying in the same hotel suite? Meanwhile, one of them is fooling around with a woman twice his age and the other one is coming on to your best friend. This is *confused?*"

Her lip trembled. "Yes. That's what I call it."

"Oh, Lizzie…"

"Okay, I listened, and I did not agree." She backed away from him, glaring from under the brim of her wide purple hat. "Saffron is my friend. She has been my friend for a very long time and she will stay my friend. I am not an enabler. I do not need a shrink. And I do not need your help."

And with one last, frustrated noise that came out something like "yeeesh," Lizzie took off.

Well, he'd made a hash of that, hadn't he?

His leg was stiff from too much sitting, and Joe winced as he stood up. Mulling over in his mind what he could've said to better convince Lizzie that she had a problem, he strolled out onto the deck, gazing at the cool, dark water of Geneva Lake.

The sun shone on the lake, and laughter rang out from the next houseboat over, where a group of well-dressed people laughed and drank exotic looking cocktails, enjoying their leisure time. Joe realized for the first time that there was something to be said for playgrounds of the rich.

But it still didn't tell him what to do about the

problem of Lizzie Muldoon. "None of my business if she wants to screw up her life," he muttered.

But he just wasn't the kind of guy who sat back and watched a person he liked go down in flames. And whatever game Lizzie and her friends were playing, the flames were already starting to crackle.

Frowning thoughtfully, Joe strode back into Viv's studio, vaguely wishing he could join the party next door instead. They seemed like they were having a lot better time.

"Oh, please." Two steps in the door, he almost turned right around and left.

As Viv whooped it up, Muscle Boy stripped off his shirt, striking a pectoral-intensive pose next to one of the smaller statues.

"Look at that six-pack," Viv said admiringly. She slid her hand over the ripples in the kid's rock-hard abdomen. "Lizzie, you have to feel this."

"Oh, it's impressive all right. I don't think I need to—"

But when Viv grabbed her hand and ran it over the "six-pack," Lizzie just giggled. Her cheeks were pink, but Joe noticed she didn't pull her hand away. He clenched his jaw.

"Y'see," Viv mused, hefting the two-foot plaster version in her arms, "Storm has it all over the guy who posed for this one. Don't you just love the play of skin and sinew, how the light kind of skims over those little knots of muscle?"

No, Joe thought, *I do not.* In fact, he thought Arnold Schwarzenegger Lite over there was a moron, and all he needed was a few women sticking bills in his waistband to start a new career. It was gross.

As Viv waved her hands in the air, outlining what she wanted to do to immortalize Storm for all time, her voice rose. "I see you ten feet tall," she cried. "Naked. Glorious. In bronze."

But Joe's eyes followed Lizzie. Slipping away from the outrageous casting session, she bumped into Zurik, who was still snarling on the sidelines somewhere. Saffron was absent for the moment, and Joe could hear every word as Zurik started in on Lizzie.

"I'm an artist," he persisted. "A real artist. I can't be expected to lie when some untalented hack asks me for an appraisal of her work. You do see that that would be like a betrayal of my entire professional life, don't you?"

Lizzie's shoulders sagged. Joe couldn't hear her response, but it looked as if she were placating that weasel. Lounging near the door, Joe narrowed his eyes.

Then the weasel had the brass to physically drag Lizzie around the big statue, the eight-footer. "Look at the size of the buttocks," he sneered. "And the thighs! It's totally out of proportion. Not to mention the pe—"

"I see what you're getting at!" Lizzie interrupted. "I don't need an inventory."

"But even if you give her the benefit of the doubt, and say it isn't art, just erotica, well, I don't think this is erotic, do you?"

Joe edged closer. Was it his imagination or had Zurik's tone changed as soon as he got Lizzie behind the big nude? His voice was softer, huskier, and he fingered her arm in a way that made steam come out Joe's ears. Who did the weasel think he was?

Lizzie seemed to be trying to listen politely, and Joe saw her send a couple of nervous glances over at Viv, who was still holding court with her boy toy.

"I get it," Joe said under his breath. "She doesn't want to knee him in the groin, because she still wants Viv to think they're a couple of lovebirds."

Joe felt ill. Whatever Lizzie's motives, Zurik appeared to be taking advantage of it. He dipped his head, looking like his lips were headed for her neck, but her floppy hat got in the way.

Joe's hands balled into fists. The little creep had just played footsie with Saffron at lunch, and now he was pawing Lizzie?

"No way in hell I'm standing around for that," Joe said between gritted teeth. It only took him a few uneven strides to wrench the painter out from behind the statue, and connect one strong fist with one weak jaw.

Joe stepped back as the weasel slipped to the floor in a heap. He grinned. Man, that felt good.

"Joe!" Lizzie cried. "How could you?"

He couldn't help a certain cocky note in his voice, could he? "He deserved it."

"Yes, he did, Joe. Good for you!" Viv yelled. "I've been waiting for someone to pop that jerk one all afternoon."

Viv might be thrilled, but Lizzie was hopping mad. "Joe!" she said again, louder and longer this time. "Violence never solves anything. And I told you I could handle it."

"He had his paws all over you and he was going

in with his mouth.'' Joe shuddered. ''Yeah, you were handling it all right.''

''What happened here?'' Saffron came careering in from wherever she'd gotten off to, letting out a shriek of distress and running to cradle the unkempt painter next to her cleavage. ''Who did this?'' She stared daggers at Joe. ''You? Why? What have you got against poor Alexander? This is criminal!''

Joe took a certain amount of satisfaction in the fact that Zurik's hair had fallen into a semblance of order once he'd had his head snapped back.

''Call the police!'' Saffron cried.

''Look, either he was cheating on Lizzie with you, or he was cheating on you with Lizzie,'' Joe informed her coldly. ''I don't care which, but I think your concern is misplaced.''

Saffron's round little mouth dropped open.

''No one's calling any police,'' Viv said sternly. ''But, Joe, maybe you better take off before that guy wakes up. I don't want another fight here. But don't worry. We'll give him a bed and a private nurse to recuperate.'' With a grimace, she crooked a thumb Saffron's way. ''I tried to warn you, Liz. If this doesn't break off the engagement, nothing will.''

Lizzie hesitated. Gamely, she announced, ''Consider it broken. I never want to see him again!'' And then she made a big show of twisting off the diamond—if it *was* a diamond—on her ring finger and tossing it at his unconscious body. It made a ping as it rolled around on the floor, where Saffron finally picked it up.

Score one for melodrama. It looked like Lizzie was back down to one bogus fiancé.

"And as for you..." Turning on Joe, Lizzie crossed her arms over her chest. "I think Viv is right and you should leave. You're, you're...out of control."

"I will be pleased as punch to get the hell out of here." His gaze was grim. "But you're coming with me."

"You know, that's not a bad idea," she said hotly. "I think you need a good talking-to about meddling in my affairs. I think you need to be told to butt out. Maybe you're an enabler. Maybe you need a shrink!"

"Maybe I do—for getting mixed up with you."

"Told you so."

They stood there, glaring at each other, until Lizzie finally slammed out the door and down the stairs. Joe wasn't far behind.

The words *I didn't even know they knew each other* came floating after them in Viv's voice.

It wasn't until they were both well on land, pounding the concrete sidewalk of the landing, that Lizzie stopped. She looked around.

"We came in a limo from the hotel. We don't have a car."

"Then I guess we'd better start walking."

His knee started to kill him less than half a mile into this ill-advised little hiking trip. He did his best to ignore it, but it was throbbing like an SOB, and it got worse every time his foot hit the pavement.

"This way," he growled, veering onto a wandering country lane. It was paved in plain old dirt, and he was hoping the change in terrain would help. It didn't.

He noticed that Lizzie eased up on her pace, plus she kept sending him worried looks, and then she started to wring her hands. "Joe, you're really limping badly. Are you having a problem?"

"Same old problem." He grimaced, biting down hard to stave off the shooting pain.

"Hold on." Looking determined, Lizzie trudged over and tried to haul his arm around her shoulders, as if she were planning to prop him up for the rest of the walk.

All it took was one brush of her warm, smooth skin against his arm, and Joe hopped backward on one foot, feeling snakebit. "Didn't we already try this once, in the swan pond? As I recall, it didn't work very well that time, either."

She stamped her foot. "Can you just accept some help for once, please, without getting all testy?"

He thought about that pot-kettle thing again, but he kept it to himself. On the other hand, there was no way he was going to make it back to the hotel without her help. And he was nothing if not a realist.

Grudgingly, he said, "Take off your hat. It's in the way."

She did it, fluffing her soft, dark waves with one hand, dangling the purple straw hat in the other.

"Okay, now come over here."

Again, she did as she was told without comment. This was a new experience for her, he felt sure.

Awkwardly, she slipped one arm around his waist, and he leaned over and braced himself on her shoulder, not noticing the sleek silk of her dress or the peach-soft skin at the nape of her neck. Nope, not noticing at all.

So if he felt a little warmer than he had before, it was from exertion, not from Lizzie standing too close, her face tipped up near his, her lips parted and moist, her eyes sparkling with desire, her breasts rising and falling with each breath, barely grazing the hard wall of his chest.

It would be so easy to kiss her, to just bend down an inch or two and take those luscious lips. And when she responded, as he knew she would, it would be so sweet and heady that he wouldn't even think about his damn leg, or her multiple fiancés, or the fact that she was the wackiest woman he'd ever met.

Lizzie stretched up on tiptoe, pressing even closer.

"I, uh… This isn't going to work." Once more, he staggered away.

"Oh, Joe, I'm so sorry," she rushed to say. "Of course, here I am, acting like I'm in a trance, and you're in terrible pain. Look, there's a big apple tree, and the grass under it looks really soft. Why don't we sit and rest under the tree for a few minutes, until you feel better?"

She fussed over him all the way to the tree, and Joe thought he just might die from all the attention, especially when she rubbed against him in ways he knew she wasn't aware of.

There were still apple blossoms on the tree, tiny white blooms, and their heady, spicy fragrance wafted down to his nose. It was sunny and breezy on this secluded country lane, and just about the perfect setting for a seduction or anything else. Especially tucked under that apple tree, with Lizzie on top of him like whipped cream on a sundae.

"Is that better?" she inquired, helping him drop to a sitting position. He extended his leg, and Lizzie had her hands all over it, massaging, soothing....

"Uh, Lizzie, I don't think that's a good idea." He held himself very still, but her hands were roaming too far up his thigh, and he wasn't sure he could be responsible for his runaway urges.

"It feels a little tight, but I think I can—" Her voice died out as she lifted her gaze, saw the heated expression in his eyes, and let out a very small, very sexy moan.

That was all it took. He'd never claimed to be a saint.

He reached for her, pulled her right into his lap, and lowered his hungry, hot mouth to hers.

She tasted delicious. Wrapping her arms around his neck, she pressed up into the kiss, as greedy and impatient as he was.

He'd kissed plenty of women in his time, but he couldn't remember it ever feeling like this, as if he were burning from the inside out, as if he would never be the same again.

It was surprising, it was fabulous, and it just about scared the pants off him.

"Lizzie," Joe breathed into her mouth. She slid her tongue across his bottom lip, weakening his resolve, but he managed to say, "We shouldn't—"

"Don't talk," she said in a ragged voice, shoving her fingers into his hair and urging him back to her mouth.

But Joe edged away. He couldn't believe he was doing this, but he couldn't stop. "I'm sorry, Lizzie, but I can't. I want you so bad it's making my teeth ache, but I can't do this with someone I don't know, someone I don't trust.''

"Oh, Joe..."

With his arms still holding her fast, he pleaded, "All you have to do is tell me the truth, Lizzie. I want you. I won't deny that. But only if you get out of whatever crazy scam you've got going with Saffron and those two losers. As long as you're trying to cheat Budge and Viv and whoever else you've targeted as a mark, I won't be with you.''

"Scam?" she repeated, incredulous, scrambling out of his lap to her knees. "Mark? You make it sound as if you think I'm a con artist. Is that what you think?''

"What am I supposed to think?''

"Maybe you should take a good look at me and see who I am." She flung her arms wide. "Take a good look. Do I look like the sort of person who would cheat other people out of their money?''

He was too desperate, too angry, to listen to any more of her excuses. So he cut her off the best way he knew how. He kissed her again.

It wasn't a nice kiss. With his lips and his tongue, with his arms locking her to him, he punished her, he fought with her, and he felt her surrender. She made that sinful, luscious moan again, melting into his arms, telling him with her mouth and her body that she would give him anything he wanted.

And that's when he pulled back. "What I want," he whispered, still trailing his lips over her neck and her cheeks, "is for you to come clean, to clear this up. I won't play games with you, no matter how..."

Framing her face with his hands, he kissed her deep

and slow one last time. "No matter how tempting those games may be." He drew his brows together darkly. "Not as long as the rest of the world looks at the two of us and sees me helping you cheat on one fiancé or the other."

Lizzie swallowed. "Y-you're jealous?" she murmured.

"Of those jokers? Please." He shrugged. "No, I'm not jealous. It's more like my honor is important to me. Do you understand that?"

"Honor?" she echoed, her dark-blue eyes growing soft and luminous with awe.

Joe groaned. He could read that hero worship stuff all over her expressive face. He hated it. But he supposed he could force himself to handle it if it would push her over the edge into being honest with him and with herself.

"I think that's beautiful, Joe," she whispered, brushing her fingertips along the edge of his jaw. "An honorable man."

He knew he had her, right there on the brink of a confession. Pulling her fingertips to his lips, he kissed them gently. "Don't worry, Lizzie. I know you didn't come up with this nonsense on your own. I know that it has to be Saffron's fault."

"Does it really matter?"

"C'mon, Lizzie, you can tell me. Is it money? Budge and Viv's money? What trouble are you in?" he asked soothingly. "Just let me handle it, and I'll make it go away."

"You'll make it go away?" she repeated in a halting tone. "You think you can make all my problems go away?"

"Lizzie, don't get the wrong—"

"Forget it," she said suddenly, jumping to her feet. "You just don't get it, do you? I have no intention of letting you or any other man jump in to try to rescue me like I'm some pea-brained damsel in distress. No way! I have never, ever allowed a *guy* to control me or my problems and I'm not starting now."

Whoa. That was an overreaction.

Lizzie crammed her hat back down over her hair, practically spitting out her words, really picking up steam. "Why, the next thing I know, you'll be telling me I have to fire my night watchman, Oliver, just because he has a slight narcolepsy problem, or Dick in Accounting, because of that silly embezzling thing," she scoffed. "And then you'll say, 'Lizzie, you really need to dress more like a normal person, so the velvet and the wedgies have got to go.' And then, you'll make me give up my vintage Bug and my funky house and my six cats and... And I won't, do you hear me? I won't give up any of who I am, for you or anyone else."

Before he had a chance to do more than blink, she charged off the grass and down to the lane. "As soon as I get to the hotel, I'll send a car back for you," she called out.

He could see her gesticulating and muttering as she trotted farther and farther away, keeping up a brisk pace that he could never hope to catch, not in this condition.

Joe sat there, stupefied, feeling like he'd just survived ground zero of a nuclear bomb. He didn't understand any of it.

Oliver the night watchman who had a slight narcolepsy problem? Giving up velvet and wedgies? How did that follow from what he'd said?

"Women," he growled, trying to get his right foot under him and hang on to the apple tree long enough to lurch himself up to his feet. "I never will understand women."

He stopped, staring after her. "Can she really have six cats?"

As Joe idled there, limping along the lane, waiting for the ride he knew would get there sooner or later, he had plenty of time to mull every nuance of the last conversation over in his mind.

What should he have done differently? Not kissed her, that was for sure. Maybe if he hadn't been thinking with his groin, he might have dealt with her more skillfully.

"Or maybe not," he grumbled. When she was going to throw in everything but the kitchen sink— night watchmen, accountants, shoes, cats, even her precious VW Bug—what chance did he have to make heads or tails of anything?

It was a given that he didn't know Lizzie that well—he'd only met her yesterday. Okay, so they were an eventful couple of days, but still…

Even on such a short acquaintance, he decided he knew her well enough to be sure she would never willingly cheat Budge or Viv or even snobby old Genevieve Knox. So he had to be right the first time—this had to be a misguided attempt to shield someone she cared about.

"Saffron," he said grimly. He was growing less

and less fond of that little twit as the minutes swept by.

A big, dark limo with the Swan's Folly crest on the side crawled down the lane, and Joe hailed it thankfully, glad to put his leg up and rest awhile. He sank into the deep leather seat, propped his leg up, took a bottle of water out of the minifridge and relaxed into the life of a rich man for as long as it took to get back to the hotel.

But as the limo drove him smoothly along, with nary a bump, he found his thoughts once more returning to perplexing, aggravating Lizzie Muldoon and the bizarre world she inhabited.

"She's lying to me," he muttered. "And I hate liars."

Usually that would've been the end of it. Life was too short to waste on game-playing fakes.

But this thing with Lizzie and her mystery men wasn't any normal lie. It was so darn weird, and Lizzie was so clearly in need of saving, he found, to his astonishment, that he was willing to make an exception.

So what could it be? What kind of trouble could she be in that having either Storm or Zurik around would fix?

Musing over the possibilities, Joe was preoccupied as the limousine pulled to a stop in front of Swan's Folly. "Thanks," he called out to the driver, already hobbling past the west wing and across the path to Thistledown, where he was staying.

He was going to sit down and maybe pop a brew,

order in a burger, until it was time to get ready for tonight's bachelor party. But it wouldn't help.

He would still be as mixed up as they came, and the reason would still be Lizzie Muldoon.

Chapter Nine

The *Truelove* was Joe's second boat of the day.

The first had been Auntie Viv's combination houseboat and studio, a modern affair with lots of nouveau yuppie touches, like a satellite dish and a microwave oven, not to mention ten or twelve large plaster statues of very nude men.

But this one was different. Joe took in the gleaming wood decks and brass rails with an appreciative eye. No, he didn't know anything about yachts. But he knew class when he saw it.

Budge had told him the story—some ancient member of Caroline's family, the same guy who started the hotel dynasty way back when, had given the *Truelove* to his wife as a gift. Ever since, it had been bobbing in the rarefied waters of Geneva Lake, not far from Swan's Folly, the most exclusive inn in the empire.

Back at the turn of the century, old "Swanee" Lambert, the hotel robber baron, had made the Folly his summer house and the *Truelove* his pleasure boat, and enjoyed a very nice life indeed at Lake Geneva.

Too bad the yacht had now turned into a smoke-filled men's club, at least for the duration of Eric's bachelor party. The posh mansions high on the bluff cast their own lights down into the water, making the yacht party seem a lot more elegant than it was, as Budge Bellamy, Hainsworth Knox and various well-heeled cronies puffed on stogies and swilled expensive Scotch under a starry sky.

Behind him, Joe could hear an occasional hoot or holler as hundreds of dollars were won and lost on poker hands, as the men hung on every punch from the slugging heavyweight boxers who filled the closed-circuit TV down in the main stateroom. Cigars, Scotch, poker, boxing—none of it really suited Joe.

Which was why he found himself leaning on the shiny brass rail and staring down into the deep, dark water.

He knew he should go try to make merry. But if this was supposed to be a celebration, nobody seemed all that happy. Especially not Eric, the groom, who was in anything but a party mood, except for a rapid consumption of Scotch.

As Kevin, Joe's much younger half brother, walked by, Joe grabbed him, glad to see a familiar face. Of all the Bellamy boys, Joe liked Kevin the best. Why not? Joe wasn't related by blood to the others. But he and Kevin shared a mother.

So Kevin might be half Budge's boy, born to the breed of silver spoons and prep schools, but his gene pool was also big enough to include plainspoken Sheila Hennessey, the mom Joe loved so dearly.

Kevin seemed to have acquired the best of both parents. So far, anyway.

"Hey, Kev, what's up? This is the first time I've seen you all weekend. Nana's had you occupied."

"Yeah, I know. I was looking for you yesterday afternoon, but Dad said you were busy with one of the bridesmaids. The brunette, Liz?" Kevin grinned. He seemed a little tipsy, which wasn't surprising. The booze was flowing pretty freely, and most of it was aged Scotch, which was heady stuff for a man of twenty-three, like Kev.

"Oh, yeah. I know her," Joe said quietly.

"Dad was pretty ticked off," Kevin continued, wagging an unsteady finger. "He said you were skating on thin ice by fooling around with this Liz woman, and if you screwed up some investment of his, he was going to kill you."

"No offense, little bro, but your dad is usually wrong." Joe wasn't smiling. "You know I like Budge, but he tends to drive pretty far off the track."

"Hey, like that's a surprise." But there was a speculative gleam in Kevin's eye. "So you're not hot for the brunette? I could go for the blonde, myself, Bianca. Man, is she all that and a bag of chips. But she's tight with Neill, I think."

"Neill?" Joe was confused. There were enough intrigues in the Bellamy-Knox bridal party to keep Melrose Place busy. "I thought Bianca was the one with the baby, and everybody thought it was Eric's."

"Eric's? You gotta be kidding."

Joe lifted his shoulders in a shrug. "It's none of my business."

A familiar, blustery voice came booming out of the darkness. "Boys, what you up to?" Budge demanded. "How come you're not belowdecks bellying up to the poker table?"

"I don't want to lose my shirt to those titans of industry down there," Joe said with a short laugh. "They can afford to part with some dough. I can't."

"It's boring, Dad," Kevin complained. "My own brothers are the only ones at this party under fifty, and they're no help at all. Eric is knocking back Scotch like there's no tomorrow, Neill is about ready to take Eric's head off, and Joe here is staring off into space. Yeah, you guys are a fun crowd."

"Where's Muldoon's partner? Storm Shrimp or whatever his name is. I made sure he was invited." Budge looked perplexed. "I just can't figure out where that boy is hiding the brains he's supposed to have. That Velvet Pig thing is making money hand over fist, so Storm must know what he's doing, but, good God Almighty, you'd sure never guess that from the way he acts. I was hoping to get a chance to cross-examine that boy tonight. Wonder where he got to."

"You invited the Muscle Boy?" Joe snorted. "Good thing he didn't show. I'd hate to have to get into my second fist fight of the day."

Budge lowered his thick brows. "Now, Joey, I told you to leave the Muldoon girl alone. It's one thing to make time with another man's fiancée, but something else entirely when the two of them are running a business together. A mighty profitable business."

"Muscle Boy is a moron," Joe said dismissively. Budge thought Storm was running The Velvet Fig, Lizzie's company? Was the old man really that blind? "Why would you think he has any impact on Lizzie's business? She is *so* obviously the brains of that outfit."

"She's just a girl," Budge interrupted, turning a rather unbecoming shade of magenta. "She can't be in charge of a whole company."

Joe shook his head. "Sometimes, Budge, you amaze even me."

"Thank you," Budge said grandly, missing the irony completely. Getting in on the nautical theme, he saluted them. "Well, I'm off, boys. Gotta make sure that son of mine is having a good time tonight, his last as a bachelor. Anybody seen Eric recently?"

"He was downstairs at the bar a second ago," Kevin told him. As soon as his father trundled off, Kevin leaned closer to Joe, a funny smile playing about his lips. "That guy, Storm? Um, I know where he is."

Not that Joe really cared, but clearly, Kevin had a story to tell. "And?"

"I, uh, set up what you might call a practical joke, on the women and their party, back at Swan's Folly." Kevin grinned again, his white teeth shining in the evening air. The kid had an infectious smile, and he knew how to use it to his advantage. "See, Caroline's mother made all the arrangements for the party, and Winnie—you know, Caroline's sister?— she's kind of a goofball, and she was complaining that her sister's bachelorette party was going to be dryer than day-old white toast.''

"And exactly what did you do?'' Joe inquired, deciding that Kevin the Merry Prankster might be a chip off the old Budge block after all.

"I got Winnie a couple bottles of booze to liven up Genevieve Knox's punch bowl, plus Win and I passed Storm a fistful of cash to convince him to jump out of a cake.'' His grin got even bigger. "Winnie said he's going to paint himself gold and put on a loincloth or something. What a hoot, huh?''

After dumping Zurik, Storm was the last "fiancé" Lizzie had left. And now he was going to be jumping half-naked out of a cake in front of a whole room full of people.... "Yeah, a total hoot.''

"Aw, come on, Joe, don't be such a drag.'' Kevin took a gulp of his drink. "They're probably having a great time back there. And believe me, that party would've been like a wake without my help.''

"You're a big help, Kev,'' Joe said darkly, patting his little brother on the arm, wondering what would happen if he pitched him overboard. Nothing too dire. Joe'd had plenty of water rescue classes. Kevin would be fine.

But what about Lizzie?

Joe's first impulse was to run back and get her out of there before she was totally humiliated by her supposed fiancé.

His second impulse was to stay out of it, remembering quite clearly that Lizzie had told him, in no uncertain terms, that she did not need rescuing.

"Did you hear something?'' Kevin asked suddenly, peering into the darkness. "I thought I heard shouting. And maybe somebody hitting something."

"Sounds like it's coming from over there." Joe pulled Kevin with him, rounding the gleaming deck just in time to see Eric take a wild swing at his older brother, Neill. "Let me guess—woman trouble."

As Eric lunged again, throwing a wide punch, Kevin got an arm around him and forced him back, while Joe cornered Neill.

Kevin, frequently the peacemaker in this family, offered calming words that had no effect whatsoever.

Neill snarled some crack, and Eric bristled right back, obviously unsteady on his feet.

"Why don't you guys chill out for a few minutes?" Joe suggested, releasing Neill. "Go smoke a cigar with your dad, have a drink, play some poker."

A scowl crossed Neill's handsome face. "Cigars stink, and so does this party," he said heavily. "Have the captain stop at the next dock."

"The captain takes his orders from me, and he's not stopping," Eric retorted.

Joe sighed. These guys just would *not* let it go, would they?

As Neill edged closer to the rail, Kevin looked startled. "You aren't thinking of jumping ship, are you, Neill?"

"Just watch me."

Before anyone had a chance to react, Neill hoisted himself over the rail and dived into the dark water below. Kevin cried, "What the hell do you think you're doing?" but it was too late to stop him. After one large splash, all they heard was the slap of water against the side of the *Truelove*.

"How much did he have to drink?" Joe asked hurriedly. He hadn't smelled liquor on Neill, but that wasn't conclusive. "If he's loaded, he may pass out in the water."

"He was fine," Eric insisted.

But Joe wasn't taking any chances. Without even bothering to strip off his jacket, he jumped in after Neill.

He couldn't see the other swimmer, but he could hear Neill's even strokes gliding through the water ahead of him, clearly smooth as silk and not in any danger.

In fact, Neill reached shore well before Joe did. As Joe emerged from the water, fully clothed and dripping from head to toe for the second time in two days, all he caught was a pair of taillights from some crazy kind of truck, disappearing down the road.

Now what? Joe refused to try walking back to Swan's Folly again—it hadn't worked the first time, had it? His leg actually felt pretty good after this impromptu session of hydrotherapy, but he wasn't planning to push it.

"Hey," he called, pounding on the window of one of the limos parked at the dock, waiting for the *Truelove* to come back. As the window rolled down, Joe leaned in. "I need to go to Swan's Folly right now. Can you take me? Trust me—those guys on the yacht won't be back for hours."

"I'm sorry, sir, but I can't help you," the chauffeur returned. "This is Mr. Bellamy's car, sir, and I have instructions to wait for him."

The man recoiled from the steady drip streaming in over his door, direct from Joe's sleeve. Joe wasn't crazy about it himself—he only owned two suits, and now one had been dipped in the swan pond, and the other one christened in Geneva Lake.

Joe reached for the door without waiting to be invited. "Isn't that lucky? I *am* Mr. Bellamy. One of them."

How about that? He got to commandeer somebody else's limousine, and he didn't even have to lie.

Stripping off his jacket, he eased into the fine leather, figuring it would repel water just fine. "Home, James," he announced. He'd always wanted to say that.

"The Folly, Mr. Bellamy?"

"Right." Joe smiled, already anticipating the end of this journey, when he could stride right into the bachelorette party.

Was it his fault he was heading for the one place where Lizzie might need to be saved?

LIZZIE DRUMMED the table with her fingers, bored out of her mind.

If Saffron had been invited, at least they could've dished Caroline's dull-as-dishwater flowered dress or her perfect pearls or her helmet hairdo. But the guest list was limited to the wedding party and relatives, which meant there was no one interesting in the least.

Lizzie herself had not worn a dull-as-dishwater outfit. No, she'd chosen this adorable little periwinkle blue slip dress, fashionably short, rather bare and quite kicky. But here she was, stuck at a bachelorette party, with no one to show it to.

The ballroom at Swan's Folly was a glittering place, with a fleet of glass doors leading into the lobby on one side, and a curving verandah all the way around the outside. Overhead, crystal chandeliers sent colorful prisms twinkling across the tables, if not much light.

To the uninitiated, this all might seem sophisticated and imposing. To Lizzie, it looked like a toned-down version of Versailles on a really gloomy night.

She'd never been to a bachelorette party before, but somehow she was hoping there'd be dirty movies and guys who thought they were too sexy for their shirts. But not tonight. Not in this cavernous hall, not with Genevieve Knox's choke hold on the reins of the party.

Gen's idea of entertainment was a string quartet playing Bach. Her carefully chosen refreshments were sugary sweet marzipan flowers, stale cake and punch, with thousands of pink and white balloons as decorations. In a final touch of total unhipness, the napkins had been printed with the words *June 18th—Caroline's Last Night as Miss Knox!*

"'Caroline's last night as Miss Knox,'" Lizzie grumbled. "If that didn't come right out of a 1914 etiquette manual, I'm the Queen of France."

The only interesting thing so far had been Nana Lambert's whispered promise to do an interpretive dance tribute to her granddaughter, something she was calling "Ode to a Bride." Lizzie couldn't wait to see Genevieve's face when her mother announced she was going to dance for the assembly. Genevieve was going to have a cow.

"I just hope Nana doesn't start shedding all sorts of other people's possessions as she spins around," Lizzie said out loud. "A watch here, a wallet there."

"Punch, miss?" the waiter inquired.

"Uh, no. No thanks." Lizzie detested punch. And there was nothing else to drink at this Soirée of the Damned, either. "Excuse me. Is there a pop machine around?"

"Across the lobby, miss. Near the business offices."

"Thank you." If she was going to go, Lizzie decided she'd better duck out now, before Nana revved up her act, since that promised to be the highlight of the evening.

After quickly rummaging around for some cash, Lizzie found the machine, fed in her dollar, latched on to a diet cola, and strolled back to the party.

"Wait just a second!" She stopped cold, her hands glued to the cold glass of the ballroom door. What in the world had happened since she left?

This was no gentle "Ode to a Bride." This was a huge wedding cake, on wheels, draped with swags of tissue and cheap paper roses. And there was a large, well-muscled man, spray-painted gold from the looks of him, gyrating in the middle of the cake.

Lizzie would've recognized that physique anywhere. It had been hanging around her suite for several days, it had bared most of itself this afternoon at Viv's, and it hung in its underwear on bus stops from St. Louis to Duluth.

"Storm?" She gulped.

She was only gone for two minutes! In that amount of time, a sedate bachelorette party had turned into "The Stripper" on wheels, and, oh Lordy, Lordy, Storm had popped out.

"Oh, no." She felt the need to sit down. She felt the need to disappear, change her name, dye her hair and start a new identity.

Things became a bit of a blur for Lizzie after that, as Storm went through an elaborate dance, making it abundantly clear to everyone present that neither dancing nor stripping was his strong suit.

After tossing tiny bits of clothing hither and yon, he finished up by yanking off his starched white collar and perching it atop Caroline's stiff, sprayed hairdo as if she were Nancy Nurse on her way to the ER. From Lizzie's position way at the back of the ballroom, she couldn't see Caroline's reaction, but she heard the gasp sound loud and clear.

"Mummy!" Caroline cried, in a wobbly voice. "What should I do?"

Genevieve looked like she was going to pass out herself. Her face was flushed, and her normally perfect pageboy was mussed and ratty. She fanned herself like crazy with one of the hand-lettered menus set so prettily at every place setting, while her niece Petsy helpfully contributed an extra breeze by flapping her own menu.

Lizzie cowered against the door, quailing at the very thought of facing anyone who might think Storm was her fiancé.

"You have to go up there," she ordered herself. But her feet wouldn't move. "Oh, God, this is terrible!"

As she watched, horrified, Storm began to tango with Nana Lambert, accompanied by a harpist who was gamely trying to coax ''Hernando's Hideaway'' out of his strings.

''Olé!'' cried Nana, snatching a paper rose off the cake and sticking it between her teeth. Having the time of her life, the old lady dipped and spun with Storm and his loincloth, managing to smear some of his golden glitter across the tiers of her lavender chiffon frock.

Lizzie felt faint. Her only hope was that the gold makeup all over his face and the dim lighting would disguise Storm well enough to keep Genevieve from recognizing him. *Who else thinks he's my boyfriend?* she asked herself desperately. ''Think, Lizzie, think!''

Okay, Petsy and Viv were on the Zurik side, and Budge wasn't here, so he didn't count. Nana, bless her deaf little heart, was still confused by the non-existent matador. That only left Winnie, who was too ditzy to care, and Genevieve, who was doing the whiskey-in-the-teacup thing again, and with any luck, was too blotto to notice anything, much less the identity of Golden Boy.

In fact, now that Lizzie took a good look around, she noticed that a lot of people seemed to be feeling no pain, which was odd when there was no booze being served. She wasn't about to look a gift horse in the mouth, however, especially if the gift horse was going to get her off the hook. Very quietly, Lizzie inched over to the punch bowl and took a good whiff.

''I think I know that smell. It's that stuff they pour

in the garbage cans at frat parties. God bless Ever-clear.''

Someone had definitely spiked the punch and then sent Storm in as an undercover stripper, completely changing the tenor of this party.

If she hadn't been waiting for the other shoe to drop—or God forbid, the gold lamé loincloth— Lizzie might actually have enjoyed this.

But there was a rip-roaring fight going on up at the front, where Genevieve appeared to be tearing into someone for unknown reasons. Lizzie hung back, but she found it tough not to intercede. She knew it could just as easily be her, and probably would be her, once Genevieve discovered Golden Boy's secret identity.

She maneuvered around until she could see who Gen was dressing down. "Oh, good grief, not Bianca again. What is Genevieve's problem?''

Lizzie wove between the ladies to get closer, and she distinctly heard Genevieve lash out at poor Bianca for trying to wreck the party by hiring Storm. Huh? That made no sense whatsoever.

"Mrs. Knox,'' Lizzie ventured delicately. "I'm sure that Bianca had nothing to do with it.'' Why would she, after all?

But Genevieve brushed Lizzie off like a flea, continuing her tirade against the blond bridesmaid.

"This is all my fault,'' Lizzie murmured, starting to panic. If she hadn't brought Saffron and Saffron hadn't brought Storm, people would not be yelling and fighting and ruining Caroline's stuffy stagette party.

As she hovered there, uncertain what to do, the

door slapped open, and Neill Bellamy, Eric's older brother, came splashing into the ballroom, dripping wet, like the Creature from the Black Lagoon. Thank goodness, he rose to Bianca's defense, returning jab for jab with Genevieve, and then escorting Bianca out of there with a minimum of fuss.

Stressed and edgy, Lizzie began to suspect that a big glass of that lethal punch might come in really handy. Gazing around, she saw that ladies were lapping the stuff up like kittens with cream, and the atmosphere in the ballroom just kept getting looser and looser.

I think I'll stay away from the punch, she decided. She felt like she should do something to get this mêlée under control, but even Lizzie ''Ms. Fixer-Upper'' Muldoon didn't have an answer for a ballroom full of pickled society matrons lining up behind Nana to do ''Ode to a Bride'' as a conga.

As Nana led this rather bizarre terpsichorean effort, Lizzie realized that Storm was nowhere to be seen. Lizzie gave the room a good once-over, not ready to relax yet, but she couldn't find him. Could she really be that lucky? Could he be gone for good, with no one the wiser and her goose uncooked?

''Phew,'' she whispered, still not sure how she'd escaped a major meltdown.

Thank goodness for free-flowing spiked punch and a low profile. It didn't hurt that their hostess, Genevieve Knox, was the most intoxicated person there.

''Oh, my,'' Lizzie murmured, wishing she had a camera just to prove to posterity that there had been an evening, once upon a time, when Genevieve Knox let it all hang loose.

But, yes, she was seeing what she thought she was seeing.

In all their mature, white-bread glory, Nana, Genevieve and Viv had decided to put on a show. Lined up, they began to belt out an off-key, off-kilter rendition of "Stop! In the Name of Love," as the oddest trio of Supremes ever, while the harpist tried to keep up.

Lizzie wasn't the only one dissolving in laughter at that point.

After the three ladies concluded their performance with one last loud, "Stop!" Nana shouted, "Who's next? Caroline, dear, this lovely young gentleman on the harp tells me he can play 'Big Spender.' What do you say?"

Caroline said no, which was a habit with her.

"I want to boogaloo," Viv broke in. "How about Hokey Pokey or Hanky Panky? Whatever you can do."

Lizzie had high hopes that this would be a solo, but it wasn't meant to be. From out of nowhere, Viv produced a partner. Storm again. Underwear Boy had turned into the bane of Lizzie's existence.

"Just when I thought it was safe to be in the ballroom..." She closed her eyes, but she had to open them again to assess the damage.

He'd wiped off most of the paint and put on pants. That might've been a welcome development, except it lost him any hope of a disguise, as he and Viv tripped the light fantastic, right there in the middle of the ballroom.

As they wound their bodies together, with not a dime's worth of distance between them, Genevieve marched over and grabbed Lizzie.

Time to face the music at last. She braced herself.

Genevieve hiccuped loudly. "Elizabeth, dear, don't you think you'd better go save your fiancé before he commits an unclean act with Vivian Bellamy right there on the dance floor?"

Lizzie came up with something in the neighborhood of "Uh, well, I, uh," as her extremely cogent reply.

On her other side, Petsy interrupted, tapping her on the shoulder. Her eyes were glassy and she seemed to be experiencing difficulty keeping herself upright. Drunk as a skunk, obviously. "The guy dancing with Viv is not Lisa's fiancé," she insisted. "I saw him. Blond, skinny, earring. Right, Lisa?"

Lizzie glanced from one to the other, unsure what to do or say, hoping against hope they were plastered enough not to remember this tomorrow. But Genevieve and Petsy got noisier and more boisterous, debating about who exactly Lizzie's fiancé was.

"It's him!" Gen shouted. "That one right there." To punctuate her argument, she poked Petsy in her bony collarbone.

Petsy shoved her right back. "It is not! It's the raggedy blond guy with the earring!"

They were actually loud enough that Nana Lambert heard them. As she tripped over, inquiring, "Who are we talking about, dears?" Lizzie found herself backpedaling, right out the door and onto the verandah.

If she wasn't there, they couldn't very well string her up, could they?

She took one step backward and then another, feeling for the door to the verandah, perilously close to freedom. Until she ran smack-dab into something hard, cold and wet.

Extending her hand, she tried to identify it. Hard, cold, wet and definitely masculine.

She spun around. "Joe?"

That was all she got out before he pulled her into his arms, kissed her thoroughly, and then heaved her up and tossed her over his shoulder.

"You can't do this," she hollered, but her voice was bouncing up and down.

"Sure I can. It's the classic Fireman's Carry. Stop wiggling."

Holding herself as still as she could, Lizzie squeezed her eyes shut, very afraid that the hem of her flirty little slip dress wouldn't quite reach to cover her bottom in this precarious position. And what was Joe doing this for, anyway, when it would probably wreck his knee again and he would fall down and they would both end up in the hospital?

Behind them, she heard Nana Lambert cry triumphantly, "*There's* Lizzie's fiancé. I told you it was the matador!"

But the sounds of the party receded behind her somewhere as she got trounced along to wherever it was he was taking her. Once they left the ballroom and hit the lawn, it was too dark for her to get her bearings, even if she hadn't been flopping up and down like a yo-yo.

"Put me down! Stop this!" She fussed and

moaned with every step, but it didn't do any good. She even hit him, but he still didn't pay any attention. Joe had become an immovable object, an irresistible force.

She was just cargo.

When Joe finally, blessedly put her down, it took a moment to clear her head enough to recognize the hall outside the Prince Siegfried Suite.

She found her voice quickly enough. "What did you think you were doing?" she demanded, ready to throw a temper tantrum out of sheer frustration. She plucked at the front of her silk georgette dress, but it was moist from contact with his soaked shirt, and sticking to her from collar to belly button. "Look what you did! I love this dress, and now it's all...wet."

"It looks great from here," he whispered. His eyes held her hotly, and he spoke in a rough, uneven tone that reached and touched her in all sorts of interesting places.

Lizzie's throat went dry. This wasn't fair. "I've had a really bad night," she continued, although she could tell she was losing all her righteous indignation. "A really bad night. I don't appreciate capping it off by being hauled around like a sack of potatoes."

"I was rescuing you from the tangle of your own lies," he told her, offering a rakish grin she hadn't seen on him before. It was adorable. "You and I both know you're not engaged to either of those clowns. So you must need a fiancé pretty bad, right? Well, I'm a better choice than either of them. If you insist on having a fake fiancé, it's going to be me!"

"No—" she began, but he just kissed her again, his mouth so hot and demanding, so provoking and delicious, that she ended up in the same pool of frustrated desire she was every time he touched her.

As her good intentions formed a puddle on the carpet, Lizzie balled her hands into fists and muttered, "I hate this. I hate myself."

Her body was a traitor; there were no two ways around it.

"If you insist on keeping up your charade," he said lightly, "I'm going to have to go back down there and tell them all what's going on. Big, fat announcement. I don't care if it does hang Saffron out to dry, since I figure this is all her fault anyway." He cocked an eyebrow. He cupped her face with one hand. "Is that what you want?"

Lizzie flared her nostrils, trying to take in more air and get some oxygen to her brain. She knew what she wanted, and it had nothing to do with truth-telling. It had to do with ripping off his clothes and licking him from stem to stern.

She paused. "I want you to kiss me again."

"Not until you tell me the truth. The complete truth."

She bit her lip, but she couldn't stand this terrible hunger, this incredible ache. "You drive a hard bargain."

"I try."

She hesitated as long as she could. But Joe was an irresistible force. "Okay," she said miserably, taking him by the hand. This had gone too far to turn back now. "Come in and I'll tell you. I'll tell you everything."

She opened the door to the suite, pulling Joe along behind her, but she had barely hit the parlor when she stopped. "Oh, God. Not again."

This time it wasn't two half-dressed men watching TV. This time it was Saffron and Zurik rolling around on the floor!

Retreating quickly, pushing Joe out the door before he saw anything, Lizzie made up her mind in a flash.

She let her gaze trail over him, from his wet shirt, plastered to his hard chest and shoulders, to his teasing green eyes and clever, tantalizing lips. Oh, he was good-looking and very sexy. No question about that. He took her breath away.

But when she looked at Joe, she also saw trust and affection and something she could really hold on to. Refuge.

In a world gone mad, Joe was the sanest thing going.

"Joe," she asked hopefully, "Can I stay with you tonight?"

Chapter Ten

She didn't need to ask him twice.

Joe had her turned around and headed to his cottage before she had a chance to think better of it. He didn't know what Lizzie had in mind, but it didn't matter. While she was pliant and cooperative, he was going to coax a confession out of her. And then, once that was disposed of, he planned to seduce her right out of her socks.

He figured she didn't know that yet. But she would soon.

He could still feel the imprint of her sweet, round bottom in that silky fabric, pressed securely into his hand as he bent her over his shoulder. He smiled to himself, imagining peeling her out of that maddening, teasing dress of hers, with its revealing lines and tempting curves, imagining himself setting the pace, calling the shots, wrapping Lizzie around his little finger, making slow, languid, mind-numbing love to her until they were both exhausted.

Anticipating the night ahead, Joe rubbed his thumb over her wrist, feeling her pulse jump against him every time he so much as brushed her skin.

Oh, yeah. This was going to be good.

With other areas of his body on red alert, he didn't have time for pain in his leg. Almost giddy, Joe began to hurry as they skirted a stand of lush, fragrant crab apple trees and crossed the last path before Thistle Cottage.

If his smile was smug, he felt entitled. Lizzie wasn't going to know what hit her. Once she was in his arms, he would never let her go. And she would be in his arms.

Very, very soon.

LIZZIE HAD TO hustle to keep up with him. She almost joked, "Where's the fire?" but worried that levity might wreck the mood.

Where in the world were they going, anyway? It was dark out here on the Folly's grounds, lit only by an occasional old-fashioned, wrought-iron lamp with a round, frosted globe. *Over the river and through the woods,* her mind sang to her.

"Where are we?" she asked, peering into the shadows of an immense stand of elms. "Are you taking me into the woods?"

"Believe it or not, my room's out here, one of these cutesy little cottages. But don't worry—it's not much farther." He grinned into the darkness, and Lizzie thought again what a truly remarkable mouth he had. She couldn't ever remember looking at a pair of lips and immediately conjuring up naughty images of what she'd like to do with them. And where exactly on her body she wanted to start.

She pretended that the reason she was huffing and puffing was that he was in such a rush. But she knew it was the night and the moonlight and the summer breeze, ruffling her slightly damp dress, creating the most interesting sensation. And Joe, wet and wonderful, with his warm, strong hand wrapped so tightly around hers.

Lizzie, think about something else, she ordered herself. *This is confession time, not seduction time. You came with him to spill your guts, not to jump his bones. And when he hears what you have to say, he may be in no mood to get cozy.*

Blast it, anyway.

When they passed a small, picturesque Elizabethan-style cottage—the charming little sign said this one was Peaseblossom—Lizzie found it a convenient distraction. She cooed, "Does yours look like this one? It's so cute!"

"Pretty much. I had a feeling you'd say that."

So far, she'd only stayed in the main building of the hotel, and hadn't really been aware of these miniature, thatched-roof bungalows scattered around the grounds. Here was Peaseblossom and there was Dandelion, tucked neatly under sweeping trees and blooming hedges, looking about as enchanting as possible without fairies and twinkle lights.

"They seem to have stuck most of the men in the wedding party out here in the back forty," Joe said with a touch of irony. "I guess to keep us out of trouble. But they're a lot too girly, if you ask me."

"I think they're perfect," she breathed.

Thistle Cottage was dead ahead, a little separate from the others. Joe had left the lights on, and you could see dainty lace curtains wafting in the windows, and a luxurious hanging basket—impatiens, maybe—with abundant leaves and flowers cascading down to the sill.

"It's very…inviting, isn't it?" Lizzie murmured, as Joe slipped his key in the door.

"I hope so." He grinned and threw open the door, guiding her in.

So why did she feel like Little Red Riding Hood after her trip to Grandmother's place, wondering what awaited inside? Only this time the Wolf wasn't going to eat her up, he was going to stand as judge and jury.

Lizzie looked around. It was quite wonderful in Thistle Cottage—all bright white wicker and comfy cushions, done in a delicate, pale green-and-lilac thistle print. There was a window seat, botanical watercolors on the walls, even the requisite television and kitchen alcove to make Thistle Cottage up-to-date for discerning guests.

Lizzie flat-out loved this place.

Since her natural inclination on this confession thing was to stall as long as possible, it didn't help that she didn't want to mar Thistle Cottage with her ridiculous story. She wanted to enjoy it, not wreck it forever in her memory.

As she pondered how to begin, Joe gave her a stay of execution. "I need to get out of these wet clothes."

Fine by me.

"It'll just take a second."

"Take your time." Her own dress was mostly dry by now, although she considered shedding it. Maybe that would get him off the confession track. But no. *Femme fatale* really wasn't her style.

Joe vanished up the stairs to what she assumed was a loft bedroom up there. He returned wearing a thick terry cloth bathrobe, with a towel around his head, and he briskly rubbed his hair.

She wanted to say, *How do you expect me to remember what I was going to say when you're dressed like that?* Instead she just tried to keep breathing.

"Well?" he said, rubbing his hands. "Do you want to sit or stand? Something to drink or eat?"

That was the first hint she had that he was nervous, too.

And when she saw that, Lizzie's strong social conscience, her need to mend other people's frayed ends, came running to the forefront. She found herself reassuring him, "It will be okay, Joe. Let's just get it over with, shall we?"

With his gaze fixed and unwavering, he nodded.

Lizzie inhaled deeply, looking for courage. She knew that the minute she started, all the enchantment of Thistle Cottage would fade away, that they would be back to judging her friends and analyzing her emotional stability, putting The Life and Times of Lizzie Muldoon under a microscope. But it had to be done.

She sat, scooted right to the edge of her wicker chair, and launched into it, quick and dirty. "It was Saffron. She started it." She raised a hand to keep him from interrupting. "And I know you knew that, but not for the reasons you think."

"I haven't been able to think of any reasons."

"Okay, well, the obvious choice was that she did it for me. Because of Eric. Because I used to, you

know, years and years ago, have a crush on him."
She smiled weakly.

"Oh, years and years ago, huh?" he asked with
a sardonic edge.

"Yes," she repeated firmly, "years and years
ago. But because of that, Saff knew I didn't want to
come to this wedding, especially not as a bridesmaid." Lizzie lifted her shoulders in an awkward
shrug, and she dug the toe of one periwinkle velvet
sandal into the carpet. "Sometimes it's hard to give
up the silly, romantic dreams you have when you're
a kid."

"And those silly romantic dreams would be...?"

"Well, me with Eric." Lizzie jumped to her feet,
needing to pace off some excess energy. "So Saffron proposed that I should come here with a fake
fiancé, to impress Eric, which was, of course, in-
credibly stupid—"

"And you went along with it?" he demanded.

Lizzie glared at him. "Of course not! I told her
no, never, not in a million years."

"But she did it, anyway?" he persisted, looking
perplexed. "And then she added an extra fiancé just
for good measure?"

"No, that's not it at all." Lizzie pushed the dark
fringe of her bangs away from her forehead with the
heel of one hand. "If you would just be quiet and
let me tell you..."

Joe sat down, folding his hands in his lap, feign-
ing temperance. "Go ahead."

After momentarily being distracted by an intriguing gap in his bathrobe just past his thigh, Lizzie
forced her eyes back to the rigid line of his jaw and

the pulse jumping in his cheek. She knew darned well his patience was a sham. Well, so was hers.

"Hang on, Joe—I'm getting there." Where was she, anyway? She shook herself, trying not to peek up his robe. It wasn't easy. "So, okay, at first I thought she only did it for me, because of the whole not wanting to look like a dweeb at Eric's wedding thing. But then what was Zurik doing here?"

"Exactly."

She sent him a dark look. "Turns out Zurik was just an accident." She explained briefly about the painting and his surprise visit to finish it. "But the damage was already done, because Saff had told anyone who would listen that I was engaged and my fiancé would be here this weekend, to set up Storm's arrival, and when Viv and Petsy saw a half-naked guy in my room, they logically thought it was him. You see?"

"I do." Joe leaned forward, and his voice grew sterner, as Lizzie followed the deep V of white fabric against his dark, muscled chest.

She looked up guiltily. "What did you say?"

"I said—I don't see why you didn't call Saffron's bluff. All you had to do was make an announcement. 'Look, this is all a mistake, I'm not engaged.' And then proceed to throw Saffron and all her accomplices out on their fannies."

There was a tiny bead of water on his neck, almost ready to drop from a soft tendril of dark hair, and Lizzie stared at it, her mouth going dry. She had visions of that wee drop, spilling over Joe's collar, slipping down his neck, dribbling down...

Was it warm in here? She cleared her throat. "What were you saying?"

"Saffron. On her fanny."

"Oh, right. Well, I—I couldn't. She's my friend. As for the other part—the denials." *Focus, Lizzie, focus.* She vaguely remembered where she was going before that silly water droplet got her off track. "I tried to deny it. You know I tried."

"At the very beginning." His lips pressed together in a thin line. "But then you went along with it. You brought Storm to the garden party, remember? And you brought both of them to the rehearsal dinner! You purposely let half the world think you were involved with one or the other. And you tried to tell me it was both. At the same time."

"I did not!" When she saw the look in his eye, she relented. "You knew I was joking."

"No, I just didn't believe you. Besides, I didn't want to think about you in a threesome," he muttered. "It wasn't good for my mental health."

"Ahh." She was actually pleased to hear that. She thought.

Now Joe rose, too, limping slightly, but pacing just as fast as she did, flashing glimpses of skin every time he took a step. Lizzie stared at the carpet, sure she was losing her mind.

"So what's the rest of it?" he asked. "If it wasn't just an image booster so you could face Eric, why all the games?"

"Because Saffron is an idiot, okay?"

Lizzie stopped, clapping her hand over her mouth. *Uh-oh.* She'd just declared that her best friend was an idiot. Talk about cold. She'd never, ever thought that about Saff before, let alone said it out loud, and not for lack of cause.

They both knew that Saffron had pulled some outrageous stunts along the way. But that was just who she was. It felt like a dagger in Lizzie's heart to say such a terrible thing, to betray her dearest friend in all the world. *Saffron is an idiot.*

"Lizzie..." Joe took her shoulders in his hands, waiting until she lifted her gaze to meet his. "It's okay. You can say that when it's true. What exactly did she do?"

"It goes back. Way back." Lizzie sagged against him, keeping her hands out at her sides, not trusting herself to test so much as an inch of his skin, as he gently stroked her hair.

This was heaven and hell at the same time. Which was, she supposed, no more than she deserved.

She continued, rapidly getting it out there. "Saff was supposed to be the one who came up with the start-up capital for The Velvet Fig. I did everything else. I wrote the plans, I designed our first product—the velvet crazy quilt shoulder bags that became our trademark—I found fabric we could afford and local women to sew, I even made up the list of potential investors. All she had to do was be persuasive enough to get Budge, Viv, Genevieve and Isabella Lambert—you know, Nana—to invest."

"And this involves your love life because...?"

"Because Budge Bellamy is almost as big an idiot as Saffron," Lizzie retorted. She backed away from his hands—she absolutely could not think when he touched her that way. *Focus, Lizzie, focus.* "Budge thought *girls* shouldn't run a business, so

Saff had the brilliant idea to come up with this mythical partner who was supposed to be my boyfriend to convince Budge to fork over. Saffron creates the fiancé, and presto, Budge signs on the dotted line."

"She didn't tell you?"

Lizzie returned, "Not a word," a bit more sharply than she'd intended.

"Lying to Budge to secure an investment—isn't that fraud?" Joe asked carefully.

"I don't know." She didn't even want to think about that. Handcuffs, jail, poverty, humiliation. What else? Feeling bereft without Joe's hands on her, and yet incapable of concentrating if she was anywhere near him, Lizzie picked up a dainty, flowered pillow, and hugged it, falling backward into the loveseat. "And if it wasn't bad enough to lie to one investor, next Saff went to see Genevieve."

Joe shook his head. "But it couldn't have mattered to Genevieve whether you had a man at the board table."

"It didn't." Lizzie laughed, a hollow sound even to her. "She just wanted to make sure I had no designs on her precious daughter's precious boyfriend. You know, Eric. What a laugh, huh?"

"Him again." Joe had a funny look on his face at that one, but she had no time to stop and psychoanalyze it.

Well, *she* thought it was ridiculous, even if he didn't. Eric may have been the crush of her youth, but he'd never given even a hint that he noticed *her*. Any worries on Genevieve's part were purely paranoia.

"So that's most of it," she concluded. "Our two

biggest investors insisted that I be romantically occupied or else no cash. And no cash—no Velvet
Fig.'' Thinking aloud, she mused, ''All these years
I thought they financed The Velvet Fig because they
believed in us. But Budge only trusted us if we had
a guy in charge, and Gen only gave us money to be
sure I wasn't going after Eric. Not exactly what
you'd call confidence in the product.''

Joe shoved his hands in his pockets. ''Saffron put
your company on the line. No wonder you weren't
thinking rationally.''

That hurt. ''I was perfectly rational. I still am.''
Most of the time. ''But what could I do? I have
seventy-three employees, every single one of them
practically unemployable anywhere else.'' She considered. ''Well, not unemployable. Not because of
anything they did. But just because other employers
aren't as—''

''As understanding as you are,'' he interjected. ''I
can add two and two, Lizzie.''

''I couldn't just blurt it all out to Budge or Mrs.
Knox when I knew what it would mean.'' She gazed
imploringly at Joe. ''I couldn't.''

''No, I don't suppose you could,'' Joe said softly,
emphasizing the *you* harder than the other words.
''Lizzie, I can understand your motives, but once it
became clear that Muscle Boy and the Weasel were
sharing the role, you had to know it was going to
blow up in your face.'' He lifted his hands, brooking
no objections. ''Come on! What do they have, the
combined brain power of a miniature poodle?''

''There are very intelligent poodles out there,''
Lizzie maintained, unwilling to go down the road of

just how stupid she had to have been to trust either of those cretins to carry her purse, let alone pretend to be engaged to her.

"Any smart poodle has a heck of a lot more on the ball than either Muscle Boy or the Weasel."

No comment.

Joe glanced up. "And what do you think Budge and the others will do if they find out it was all a scam?"

"Pull out their money pronto. No one likes being made a fool of, especially not rich people. And if they back out, The Velvet Fig is DOA."

"I'm sorry, Lizzie."

But sorry wasn't enough. "That's why you have to let it be," she begged, "just long enough for me to figure out what to do about Budge and Viv and the others. Joe, I did what you wanted. I told you the truth. Will you promise to keep quiet for the time being?"

She could see him considering his options. Finally, he said, reluctantly, "For the time being."

"Thank you!" she cried, leaping over and hugging him. It was a purely spontaneous action, and she paid no attention to the warm, tingly feel of his skin under her fingers. Not even a flicker. "I know it's a lot to ask, and I know this whole thing makes me sound like a bimbo and a doormat and all the other things you accused me of, but you do understand, don't you?"

"No." Joe bracketed her face with his hands. "I tend to err on the side of honesty. It's a lot easier to pull off. You're going to have to tell your investors the truth sooner or later, you know. Frankly, I'm amazed you've kept it going this long."

"Me, too." Lizzie ran her thumb down the nubby collar of his bathrobe, allowing herself to relax into him, just for a second. "This scheming and juggling and hiding…" She shuddered. "It is *so* not me."

"Good," he said, and then he covered her mouth with his for a kiss that was much too brief to suit her. "I'm glad you're going to fess up, Lizzie. It's the best thing."

She had the feeling he was going to pull out a timetable and get her to sign off on her exact Moment of Truth next. But instead he disentangled himself, strolling casually to the phone on the desk.

He started flipping pages in the service guide, glancing up to ask, "Listen, you hungry? I'm starved—the cigar smoke on that yacht was so thick it wrecked my appetite. And I haven't seen you eat anything yet this weekend. How do you feel about room service?"

"Room service would be great," she said slowly. *Hmmm…* That was odd. Just when she thought he should've been free to put on the moves, he backed off. Honor again? Waiting till after she stood on a mountaintop and confessed each and every one of her sins?

How unpleasant of him.

As he ordered a few things and they sat back to wait, she reflected that it was disappointing he had cooled off, but she could handle it. After all, when she'd asked if she could stay with him tonight, she didn't plan for anything more than that to happen.

She didn't expect them to spend the night entwined in each other's arms or anything.

Did she?

As late evening turned to late night, a breeze began to blow the curtains at Thistle Cottage, and a full moon peeked through the trees. Lizzie hugged herself, smiling mistily out into the darkness.

"There's magic out there tonight," she whispered. Midsummer magic. Her mother believed in it totally—even left saucers of milk and honey out for fairies on nights like this.

Lizzie turned away from the window. Joe wasn't watching, but he looked up to catch her gaze. Something about the way his face softened made her heart catch. She beamed at him.

The moment she met Joe, she wondered if there might be karma or destiny at work between them. She'd never felt that way before, but what could she think, when she set out in her car and ran into Regular Joe, just her type, a real-live hero who made saving people a way of life? His idea of rescue went even further than hers did. Every day, he faced fiery rescues, whereas she just gave out jobs.

But this destiny thing... Each time she'd ventured into really deep water at Swan's Folly, hadn't Joe been there to lend a hand? What could that mean, but Fate tossing him in her lap, saying, *Wake up and pay attention, Elizabeth Rose Muldoon, this one's for you?*

She had the sudden idea that she had been fighting the wrong battle. She wasn't supposed to avoid Joe, or yell at him, or stand on ceremony, not even give in and play it his way. Maybe Fate was throwing

her to him as much as vice versa. Maybe Joe needed
her to rescue him, too, to interject a note of unpre-
dictability into his life, to knock him off balance and
keep him there.

She and Joe were fated to be together. Now all
she had to do was convince him.

"You're looking starry-eyed," Joe said suspiciously.

"I love midsummer, don't you?"

"Sure. What's not to like?"

"Mm-hmmm." Feeling marvelously unburdened
and entranced, Lizzie perched on the window seat.
"I'm so glad I told you, Joe. I feel so much better."

"Glad to hear it."

His emerald eyes narrowed on her, as if he
couldn't quite figure out what was up. Lizzie just
smiled, secure in the knowledge that she had this
round down cold.

She was sure. Her heart was so full, it made her
want to tell everyone, including the room service
boy who came knocking. But Lizzie kept her romantic notions to herself, grinning at the boy as he
wheeled in a table set up with ice-cold milk, brownies and chocolate chip cookies.

She took one look and just about started tap dancing. If she'd needed proof of her theory, here it was.
Left to his own devices, did Joe order cheeseburgers
or steak or any of the other hideous things he probably really wanted?

No. He ordered brownies and chocolate chip
cookies with milk on the side, which happened to
be Lizzie's favorite thing in all the world.

Destiny was calling out her name loud and clear.

"Joe," she said, taking a big bite of brownie and chewing very slowly, tasting every morsel. She patted the cushion next to her and winked at him. "Why don't you come and sit by me?"

He closed the door behind the waiter, and slowly, cautiously, joined her.

This was kind of fun. Very enlightening. She couldn't recall ever purposely setting out to seduce someone before, but then she'd never felt the power of destiny on her side. Guys were so easy, anyway. It was like shooting fish in a barrel to slip off her shoes and slither her foot, ever so slowly, up and down his bare calf. It was like taking candy from a baby to feed him a bite of cookie, to lick her fingers, to brush a crumb from his lip, to follow her finger with her mouth, to fling plates and cookies every which way as she knocked him to the floor and slid her body on top of his.

Besides, he was only wearing a robe. How long was he really going to hold out?

"Lizzie..." He tried to rise, but he was blocked as she pressed her hot mouth to his collar bone. "Will you hold on a minute, please?"

Lizzie sighed and sat back on her haunches. Since she was resting on his thighs, it wasn't a bad place to be. "I know what you're going to say. You're going to say you want to take it slow and you'd rather be in control and yadda, yadda, yadda. But, hey, Joe, you know what? You don't always get to be boss. You're the one who charged into the ballroom and dragged me out like a caveman. That would be *you* as the caveman, not me."

He did not look amused. "Got it."

But Lizzie was on a roll. Pent-up frustration, mid-summer madness—it was all loosening her tongue. Besides, she was convinced she was right. "Okay, Joe," she began, "so you forced the issue and you came and carted me out of the party, and I asked, 'Joe, can I stay with you tonight?' and you said 'Sure.' Now, maybe you were thinking stay with you as in *stay* with you, wink, wink, nudge, nudge, but I wasn't." She paused, folding her arms over the skimpy bodice of her slip dress. "You *were* thinking that, weren't you?"

It was clear from the look on his face that he was.

"Aaah. You wanted to seduce me. But you want to do it your way, and you don't want me jumping the gun, is that it?"

More difficult to read. But she thought she had him. "Well, I wasn't thinking about that at all. Slow, fast, my way, your way. Not at first. But then you were sitting there all night in your damn bathrobe driving me nuts, and you know what?"

"I was?" he asked, in a husky voice that sent shivers up her spine. He caught her hand.

"Was what?"

"Driving you crazy." He brought her hand to his lips, brushing one soft kiss into her palm.

"Oh, yes." Lizzie breathed deep of cool summer air. The breeze smelled like apple blossoms, mixed with the rich chocolatey odor of brownies, and a special fragrance she couldn't put her finger on. Nighttime, perhaps. Nighttime and Joe Bellamy. Who could resist thinking about love and romance on a night like this? "So you see, Joe—"

But she had no chance to finish. He sat up, he flipped her over, and now he was on top.

"I knew it," she whispered.

His lips traced the slope of her neck, and his teeth nipped her earlobe ever so gently. "Knew what?"

"That you just wanted to be in charge. To set the rules. Mmm…" She dropped her head back to the carpet, finding it difficult to breathe when his lips trailed lower, just over the rise of her breast.

"And if I do?" he asked negligently. "If I want to slow things down, to make you wait, to make it good…"

"Well, Joe." Lizzie giggled, curving an arm around his neck, pulling him down. "You don't always get what you want."

And then she slipped her free hand inside his robe, lingering on his hard, sinewy chest, exploring as much of his hot, slick skin as she could reach.

"Lizzie," he warned.

But she had destiny on her side, didn't she? Pushing his robe aside, she pressed her mouth up into his, reckless and fast, and angled a leg around him, urging him to hurry, expiring of heat and passion that couldn't, wouldn't wait. She knew he was as turned on as she was—he felt like a firecracker under her searching fingers.

His mouth was still wet and warm on hers as he hooked a finger under one skinny strap of her dress, rolling it off her shoulder. And then the other.

She rose slightly, edging him up and back, knowing full well that gravity would help her, and her slip dress would slide right down. And it did.

Joe made a sort of growl low in his throat, and she knew she had him.

"Lizzie," he murmured, his voice low and rough with desire. He bent to taste her, to test one eager nipple with his tongue and his teeth, to tease the other with his fingers, and she arched into his hand and his mouth, both at the same time, moaning with pure pleasure.

He pulled her full into his lap, where there was nothing left between them but the thin silk of her panties, and a pool of periwinkle georgette. She rocked against him, exulting in the feel of him, rigid and blazing hot underneath her.

Joe's arm tightened behind her, and he held her very still. "You win," he said darkly. "There's no way in hell I'm taking this slow."

Triumph and desire clouded her brain, and Lizzie began to move in his lap, wriggling even closer, wrapping her legs around his waist to hold him fast.

"There's also no way in hell I'm doing this on the floor."

With her cradled to the front of him, Joe rose in one smooth motion, only a little unsteady when he put his weight—and hers—on that rickety knee. "Hold on," he breathed into her ear, but his arms were fast around her, and she felt safer than she'd ever felt before.

Joe took the stairs swiftly, finding her mouth, kissing her deep and sweet as he switched on the light, kicking the door closed, and practically tossing her onto the big brass bed.

"Who is seducing whom here?" she asked breathlessly.

"Does it matter?"

"Not anymore."

And then Joe was next to her on that beautiful bed, pressing her down into the linens, murmuring soft words and touching her, caressing her, making her want to laugh and cry at the same time.

Her whole body vibrated with tension and sensation, exquisite and agonizing at the same time. She was so ready for him, she couldn't breathe, couldn't think, couldn't take one more minute of this dazzling, mind-numbing desire.

Still he waited.

But Lizzie had had enough. Pushing him backward into the bed, she climbed onto him. He only laughed, edged away, tried to play the same game of elude and delay.

This time, she meant to have her way. Lizzie poised herself, found him, slipped down, and took him with reckless abandon, moaning greedily.

Underneath her, Joe arched, fighting her, battling her for control. She didn't care. It was glorious and wonderful.

He spun her over, and she held him tight as he stroked deep inside, smooth and powerful. There he was, inside her, around her, everything she'd ever needed.

"Lizzie," he cried, and found his release, as she toppled, too, exhausted and replete.

"That was amazing," she murmured, stroking his cheek, nestling close to his steady heartbeat.

"Next time," he said, tightening his arms, "next time I start out on top."

"Who says?"

"I say."

"Control freak."

"Pot, meet the kettle."

"Forget it," she insisted. "You don't get to choose all by yourself."

"You forget it."

Lifting her head, Lizzie smiled into Joe Bellamy's beautiful, infuriating face. This kind of argument could last all night. If she was lucky.

Chapter Eleven

Saturday: Anything can happen at a Bellamy wedding

"Joe, wake up. Wake up, do you hear me?" Lizzie leapt out of bed, squinting at the clock, scanning the floor for signs of her dress.

She was not a morning person in the best of times, and after last night's hijinks, well, she was making no claims to be at the top of her game. What a mess. She was late. He was late. And where in blazes had her dress run off to?

"Thank heavens. There it is." After dragging it out from under the bed, she had just managed to fling it on over her head by the time Joe began to stir. Quickly, she ran a hand through her hair so she didn't look like something the cat dragged in on her first Morning After with the man of her destiny.

"Mmmph," he said drowsily.

"Oh, good." She beamed down at him fondly, dropping a small kiss behind his ear. "I'm really glad to see that you're not a morning person, either. That is going to be so helpful later. Because I would really hate it if you were all perky in the morning, wanting me to up eating pancakes at the crack of dawn or something. Destiny!'' she concluded happily. ''It knows what it's doing.''

''What the hell are you talking about?'' he growled.

''Morning?''

''But why? Wouldn't you rather sleep in it than talk about it?''

''Yes, actually I would.'' A lazy smile curved her lips. ''Especially after last night.''

''Oh, yeah.'' He looked pretty pleased with himself as he stretched back into the bedclothes, raising one arm over his head. ''Last night. You sure you don't want to climb back in here and try out some new tricks?''

With the sheet dipping to his waist, baring the hard planes of Joe's gorgeous chest to the hazy light of morning, Lizzie found herself tempted. Very tempted.

''No, I can't,'' she said finally, forcing her eyes away. ''I have to be at the wedding breakfast in half an hour, and I'll never make it if I jump back in there with you.'' She stopped. ''Where the heck are my shoes? Do you remember seeing my shoes?''

''Downstairs.'' He rose partway, wrapping the sheet around him, looking a shade superior and smug. ''Definitely downstairs. You were trying to seduce me and you took off your shoes and rubbed your foot up and down my leg. My bare leg.''

She tried to remember to keep breathing. ''I, uh, think I remember that.''

''Good.'' The flames from his gaze flickered over

her, warming her, too. "So what's this all about? Why are we up again?"

"Wedding breakfast. All of us lucky wedding party folks are supposed to be there. And after last night..." She groaned. "You remember—Storm and the bachelor party and Genevieve doing 'Stop! In the Name of Love.'"

"You're kidding, right?"

"'Fraid not." Lizzie couldn't quite believe it herself. "Everybody was nuts last night. Saffron and Zurik rolling around on the floor, Neill Bellamy looking like the Creature from the Black Lagoon, Storm spray-painted gold and wearing a loincloth, Gen and the Supremes number, and then, of course, me and you..."

Her face flushed with heat just thinking about it, and she felt something deep inside her coil and uncoil. Sense memory.

It was arousing, disturbing.

Oh, dear. She really had better get out of here before she did something dangerous.

"You see, because of all that, because I'm not supposed to be here with you—not yet, anyway—I have to go to the wedding breakfast." She bit her lip. "I'm really afraid of fallout from the Storm-in-the-cake thing. So I think I have to be there to deflect inquiries."

Joe slumped, yawning. "Sharing breakfast with a bunch of surly rich people with hangovers? I'll pass."

"Well, when you put it that way..." She reached for his hand. "I was kind of hoping you'd be there. I could use the support."

"Well, when you put it that way…" Joe smiled. "I'll be there." He tugged at her hand, catching her, reeling her in, dumping her into his lap.

Ooops. What a very naughty boy. "You *are* up early this morning," she breathed huskily, wiggling against his hips. She had started the motion to try to propel herself out of there, but it was definitely making things worse. Talk about aroused and dangerous.

"See what you're missing?" He cupped her bottom, sliding back and forth. "C'mon, Lizzie, come back to bed. I'll let you be on top. Promise."

"Don't do this to me, Joe," she sighed, sternly pushing herself up and out of the brass bed. "I have to go."

Leaning back against the brass rails of the headboard, Joe held up his hands. "All right. Get out of here. I'll see you later."

"Bye." Afraid she would change her mind if she lingered even a second more, Lizzie shot down the stairs, grabbed her shoes, and then raced back up again.

Joe hadn't moved. He raised an eyebrow. "Forget something?"

"I, uh…" This was so awkward. "I wanted to tell you… I mean, I thought you should know…"

"Uh-huh?"

"Joe, I just wanted to make sure you knew," she rushed to say, "that I do not jump into bed with every guy I meet, especially the way, you know, it happened here, where I kind of took matters into my own hands, so to speak."

A hot blush swamped her from head to toe. *Took matters into my own hands?* Did she really say that?

"Lizzie, I know—"

"No, no, you don't. What with the suite and the naked men and everything, you might think something very different." She was quite serious about this, and she hoped she was impressing that upon him. The last thing she wanted was for Joe to feel like some fly-by-night, run-of-the-mill conquest, one more notch in the belt of Lizzie Muldoon, Scarlet Woman.

"Lizzie, I don't think you—"

"Whatever you do or don't think, here's the deal. I have never shared anything more than conversation with either Storm or Zurik," she explained hastily, "and I'm really sorry that now people may think you're a chump for getting involved with a woman who has two other fiancés on ice back in the Prince Siegfried Suite. I know your honor and dignity are important to you, and I don't want anything I've done to cast any reflected embarrassment on you." She twisted her hands together, dangling her periwinkle velvet sandals.

"I'm not worried," Joe said calmly. "All we have to do is tell the truth. Truth is good."

"Okay, well, normally I'd agree with you," she hedged. "But, you know, if I just come right out and tell Budge and Genevieve that Saffron and I have made fools of them, they'll pull their money out of The Velvet Fig so fast it'll make your head spin."

"Is their money really worth all these lies?"

"Joe!" she cried. "We went through this last

night. You know—seventy-three employees? Remember? There's Dick the embezzler, Oliver the napper, GiGi with the speech impediment, Yvonne the hypochondriac, and I didn't even tell you about Esmie, who is very nice, but always away from the office because she likes to take her mom, who has some sort of chronic *thing,* on cruises, and she has to visit her daughter, who has led a very troubled life, at the state pen."

"Lizzie, no more." Joe swore under his breath and sank down into his pillow. "I remember. Trust me. Down to the seven cats and the velvet slippers."

"It's six and they're wedgies."

"Close enough." Tersely, he added, "The point is, Lizzie, that you need to stop letting people take advantage of you. Did you ever think that maybe Ivan and Donald and all the others would be better off if you let them stand on their own two feet and live their own lives?"

"I don't have time to discuss this right now."

"Lizzie, face it—you're a meddler and a rescue freak." Although he had not chosen the kindest turn of phrase, she could see the compassion and clarity in his sea-green eyes, and she couldn't take offense. "You really need to rethink—"

"Not now, Joe. Not now. But I'll think about it," she promised. "Really. See you at breakfast then, okay? Now, Joe, I really *do* have to go."

She leaned down and kissed him fast and hard, trying to tell him with her lips what she couldn't seem to find words for.

You are my destiny, Joe. And you may be right about me. More right than I care to admit.

The words she hadn't said aloud echoed in her thoughts as she tiptoed furtively across the lawn and the gardens, sneaking all the way around to the far side of the east wing.

You are my destiny, Joe. And maybe my destiny is to learn not to be needed quite so much.

Later. She would think about it later. Not now, when she just wanted to wrap last night's memories around her for a few more minutes.

Not being a morning person, she couldn't recall the last time she was up and outside at this time of day. That made this morning—this misty, pink-tinged dawn—even more special and unique.

"Is morning always like this?" she wondered, drinking in the lively chirping of the birds, the tickle of wet dew under her bare feet, the way the morning light shone soft and radiant over the crumbled ruins of the Folly. It was lovely. It was as if the sun and the sky and the grass knew how happy and well-loved she felt, and they were sending their best wishes. "Maybe I should do this more often."

Stifling a yawn, she eased through the French doors into the library, keeping an eye peeled for early risers who might think it was odd to see her lurking around in last night's dress.

"Home free," she muttered, making her way through the shadows of the deserted library. "One quick turn and the elevator is mine."

Lizzie pressed the brass button hard, as if that would help it get there faster. Heavens, but she was tired. And there was no time to rest now. She barely had time to dash upstairs, jump in the shower, throw on whatever clothes she could find first, and get to the stupid breakfast.

She was mulling over her tight schedule when she heard voices approaching, coming from the morning room, which was where she would be headed after she changed. Budge Bellamy, from the bombastic sound of it. The worst possible scenario.

Lizzie rammed the button again. "Get here, damn it."

There was no way she could make it to the curving staircase before they arrived. And nowhere to hide. The elevator was her only hope.

"Daddy, I wanna feed the ducks!" a small, petulant voice cried. "There's ducks in the pond. I saw. Gimme some bread. Now!"

The footsteps and the voices grew louder. Just as Lizzie gave up hope and tried desperately to think of some excuse to cover why she would be wandering the halls at 7:00 a.m. in a cocktail dress, the elevator thumped into place.

She drew back the caged door, vaulted in and shrank against the back wall with only seconds to spare, as Budge and his daughter trotted past unawares, babbling on about the ducks.

"Listen, baby-doll," Budge barked, "they probably have leftover bread in the restaurant. We'll get you some and you'll be feeding those duckies in no time."

"I wonder if I should go back and warn them," she found herself saying as the elevator lurched its way to the second floor. "They're swans, not ducks, and they can be dangerous. A small child should not be feeding them by hand."

Clonk. That was her clue that she had hit her floor.

"Lizzie Muldoon, did you hear yourself?" she demanded as she skated over to the Prince Siegfried Suite. "Budge is the one person you can't afford to run into, and yet you want to go grab him by the lapels and give him poultry-feeding advice!"

Maybe she was just tired. Or maybe Joe was right and she *was* a meddler and a rescue freak.

Words to ponder.

As she let herself into the suite, she sent up a wish that no one else would be up yet, and she could get in and dressed easily. It was a vain hope.

In fact, the place was a madhouse. Zurik wandered past her one way and Storm the other, while Saffron came stumbling out of the kitchen. Some person or persons had ordered one or more room service breakfasts, there were wet towels, dirty dishes and discarded pieces of clothing everywhere, and Lizzie wanted to scream.

"I left a warm bed in Thistle Cottage for *this?*"

"Don't talk so loud," Saffron mumbled. Her auburn curls were a tangled mess, and she had an ice bag tipping over her forehead. "We were up kind of late."

"Yes, I know. I saw you and what's-his-name going at it like greased weasels on the floor last night." Lizzie set her hands on her hips and glowered. She was not terribly familiar with glowering, but she found she kind of liked it. "I guess you were too busy to notice me or Joe, standing there, about ready to barf."

"Huh? Uh, no. I didn't see you."

"Well, I saw *you.*" Trailing her partner into the

bedroom, which looked even worse than the parlor, Lizzie picked up speed and volume. "I saw more of you than I care to remember, as a matter of fact. I also saw more of the Underwear Boy than I needed to. Are you aware he was parading around in a gold lamé loincloth last night? He did a strip show, Saffron. A strip show!"

"Really? That's weird." Saffron blinked. "Why would he do that?"

"Is that the best you can offer?" Lizzie asked, shoving aside a potato chip bag and a couple of empty beer cans so she could sit on the edge of the bed. "You know, I have been trying really hard to keep this farce of a fiancé thing going, putting what I wanted on hold, lying to Joe, and hating every minute of it. And Storm blows it all by stripping at the bachelorette party! So I'm sorry, but it's over."

"Huh? What's over?" Saffron asked dimly.

"All of it."

"Huh?"

"Saffron, if you say 'huh' one more time, I'm tossing you and your brother off the widow's walk on the top of this crazy place!" Lizzie took a deep breath. "You send him home, do you hear me? It's over. He has to leave."

"Storm?"

"Yes, Storm! You can stay, for the time being, but you'd better stay out of my way, because I don't want to see you. Any part of you. Because you've behaved disgracefully." On a roll, Lizzie finished up with, "Worse than your idiot brother, which is going some!"

"Lizzie!" Saffron wailed, but her senior partner was resolute.

"Oh, and Saff, just so you know, your new beau isn't staying, either." And then she stalked through the living room, into the other bedroom, stuck a finger in Zurik's face and announced, very precisely, "I do not care if the wedding painting is ever finished, because you are. Get your things packed up and take a hike."

"You can't do this," he started to say, but she was already gone, sneezing her way back to the parlor.

How odd. She felt positively triumphant. "Maybe there's something to be said for laying down the law, for being inconsiderate and uncooperative."

Everybody else did it. Why shouldn't she?

After digging under a stack of magazines and jumbled shoes to find her suitcase and pointedly ignoring a weeping Saffron, Lizzie retreated to the bathroom to try to get herself together.

The phone in one of the bedrooms was ringing off the hook, but she tuned it out. All around her, she could hear signs of fake fiancés leaving the premises, and it was music to her ears.

She actually sang in the shower—"Embraceable You," which reminded her of dancing with Joe— and she thought she detected a glow when she gazed at herself in the mirror. "Maybe you get to glow when you give in and grab your destiny," she told her reflection.

After donning a simple white T-shirt and a long, black linen overall jumper, she was pleased with her appearance, and proud of herself for pulling things together at the last possible moment.

She was still humming "Embraceable You" on her way down to breakfast. "I get to see Joe again," she whispered, feeling a major tingle. Would he already be there when she got there? Wait until she told him about booting out most of her roommates, kicking their sorry behinds out on the street. He was going to be thrilled.

Everything was terrific until she walked through the doors to the morning room and saw poor Eric. He huddled next to the door, quite alone, with the breakfast buffet and a gaggle of people beyond him.

"Hi, Liz," he said, exhaling deeply, staring into space, looking for all the world like some character from a depressing Swedish movie.

But this was all wrong—Lizzie had always imagined Eric stepping right out of a caper movie, one of the kind where people sipped champagne at Monte Carlo. He was supposed to conjure up images of Cary Grant, not Ingmar Bergman.

"You look terrible," she told him, gazing up at his handsome face with concern. Eric was always immaculate, but not this morning. His clothes were rumpled, his face seemed to have acquired a grayish hue, and his baby-blue eyes were red-rimmed and puffy. "What did you do last night, throw yourself under a train?"

"Wish I had. It was the bachelor party," he mumbled.

"Yikes. I always thought those things were a terrible idea. Now I'm convinced. It seems like half the people at your bachelor party ended up soaking wet, and the other half spent the night in a Dumpster somewhere.'' She drew Eric aside, setting a cool hand on his forehead to see if he was coming down with something. But he felt fine. She whispered conspiratorially, ''Has Caro seen you this morning? She's not going to be happy.''

He snorted. ''When is she ever happy?''

''Oh, Eric.'' She felt a rush of concern and dismay. Glancing around to make sure none of the Knox women were eavesdropping, Lizzie said carefully, ''We talked about this before, so you know what my advice is. If the wedding is making you this unhappy, you shouldn't go through with it.''

''Lizzie?''

''Yes?'' She gazed at Eric, thinking that once upon a time, standing this close to him would've turned her into a bowlful of jelly. Now, she just felt sorry for him. What a difference a date with destiny made. Now that she knew where and with whom she belonged, she saw Eric more clearly. He was a dear, sweet man, but one who really needed to make up his mind. She squeezed his hand. ''What is it, Eric?''

''Lizzie...''

''Yes?''

''Behind you—my stepbrother Joe is trying to tell you something.''

''What?'' Lizzie spun around. *Uh-oh.* Joe was all the way on the other side of the morning room, backlit by the light streaming in the cathedral windows. He'd been blocked from view by Budge and his wife Candy-Wanda-Brenda when she arrived, but she wasn't sure she would've seen him, anyway, occupied as she was with Eric. Baring his teeth at her, Joe looked furious. With her?

"I didn't do anything," she said out loud.

But when he sent her an exaggerated mime signal, she understood the slashing hand across the throat perfectly.

Nix on the conversation with Eric.

She crisscrossed her hands back and forth, in the universal *you don't know what you're talking about* semaphore.

But Joe persisted. *Tell them*, he mouthed. *The truth. It's time.*

This was followed by a series of bizarre gestures that Lizzie picked up amazingly well. Either she had ESP, or his version of *Tell these people that you are not engaged or living in sin with anyone, and leave Eric alone in the meantime* was very well done. Whatever—she got the message.

"I can't," she said primly, doing the zip-across-the-lips thing herself. Good heavens. Like all this gesticulation stuff wasn't suspicious!

"You sending me signals?" Budge roared. "Where's that man of yours, Lizzie? I need to talk to him."

The lie rose to her lips so easily. "Gone!" she called back. "Business."

Budge lowered his brow and shook his head, stomping off to cause trouble with some other lucky breakfast guest.

I should've told him the truth, she said under her breath. But as she looked around the room, she saw Saffron sniffling into her orange juice and bending Winnie Knox's ear, no doubt lamenting the loss of her painter pal; Genevieve and her assistant, Anne, both looking like they had tramped to Siberia and back this morning; and right here, inches away, Eric wrapped in a shroud of misery.

The minister, who should've been kicking off this breakfast with a prayer for the future happiness of Caro and Eric, was nowhere to be seen, and neither were Bianca and Neill, bridesmaid number two and the best man. Could things get any worse?

Surely Lizzie's announcement could wait until things were more settled. She wasn't sure whether it was really her social conscience, that driving need to have everyone be happy, or just cowardice. But she knew she had to put it off a little while longer.

Okay, so she knew Joe was angry, and she wished he wasn't. But the clenched jaw and malevolent glare were plenty clear.

"I can fix that later," she muttered to herself. "He promised me time, didn't he? So I'm taking my time. But right now..."

She bit her lip, glancing back at Eric. His humor had not improved in the last three seconds.

"Listen, Eric, why don't we sit down? The minister's not here yet, anyway, so we have a few minutes." She patted his arm kindly. "Why don't you fill me in on exactly what's bothering you."

He didn't say much, just sipped black coffee and grumbled something about his magazine and a botched-up story and Caroline being on his back all weekend, and Genevieve Knox having him followed.

"She did?" Lizzie gasped. "She had you followed?"

He didn't answer directly, retreating to a different topic. "Did I ever tell you how I got engaged?"

"Um, no. Not that I recall."

"Caroline got tired of waiting for me to ask her to marry me. She just announced it, all by herself." He ran a shaky hand through his hair. "What could I do? I had to go along."

"I have learned," Lizzie confided, "in my personal experience, going along with other people's plans that you want no part of, just to be nice, well, it's a really bad idea. You have to nip those things in the bud."

"Now you tell me."

Now I tell myself. "Eric, I know this is none of my business, but, well, is there someone else you *are* in love with?" She was thinking about Bianca and the mystery baby. She just had this funny feeling that Eric wouldn't be this messed up if there weren't another woman in the picture. "I won't say anything, but you should know, for yourself. Is there someone else?"

"Yes. Maybe. I'm not sure."

It didn't sound good. "For what it's worth, I can tell you this. If you don't want to marry Caroline, if you're not absolutely sure, if you can't imagine not eating, sleeping and breathing her for the rest of your life, then you have no choice, no matter how many engagements she announces." Lizzie stood up, feeling strong and clear. Out of the blue, she realized she had just clarified for herself how she felt about Joe. *Eating, sleeping and drinking Joe for the rest of my life...* It wasn't a choice—it was what had to be. "If you can't say that about Caroline, then you have to walk away."

Eric groaned and put his head in his hands.

"C'mon, it won't be that bad." She dipped down to whisper in his ear. "Just between you and me, I think it would be a lot easier to dump Caroline at the altar than it would be to wake up with her every morning."

Eric looked terrified.

"It was a joke," she tried to tell him. "Oh, well." Looping an arm around him, she gave him a nice, warm, comforting hug, bundling up all the sticky feelings she'd had for him over the years, and disposing of them in one fell swoop. "No matter what," she whispered, "all I ever wanted was for you to be happy."

"Thanks, Lizzie."

For the first time, she thought Eric Bellamy, the dream of her youth, might actually be seeing her for who she was. She beamed. "You're welcome."

She almost missed Joe brushing behind her, departing the breakfast in a hurry. But that same physical awareness, that now familiar spark of connection and chemistry and karma, jolted her as he sped by.

"Excuse me, Eric, but there's something I have to take care of." And she ran after Joe, out the morning room door and into the fresh summer day.

His long strides put him well ahead of her, and Lizzie found herself sprinting to catch up, reaching him as he crossed the terrace and veered toward the west wing. Down below, near the Folly, workmen were already putting up the chairs for this evening's wedding, and there was a clatter of activity and commotion.

"Looks like your knee must be better," Lizzie called out to Joe. "You're hardly limping at all."

"Exercise," he said tersely. "I got a workout yesterday."

"Oh, is that what you're calling it?"

His dismissive gaze swept her. "I meant the swim after the bachelor party."

"Joe," she ventured, catching his sleeve, "don't be mad at me. I'll tell them about the fake fiancé thing as soon as the wedding is over. I promise. I told you I didn't want to do it right away. I thought you were okay with that."

All he said was, "It doesn't matter. You got into this mess because you let Saffron and then Zurik and then Storm walk all over you. You're a doormat."

"A doormat? But I—" she started, eager to tell him about banishing the men already this morning.

"You wouldn't even be at this wedding if you'd told Caroline to take a hike like you should've when she first asked you. You don't like her. You're in love with her groom. It's ridiculous to stand up at her wedding."

"In love with Eric?" she stammered. "You can't be serious."

He kept on going, not listening, slamming one foot in front of the other. Could his knee take all this stress?

"Are you going to hurt yourself, the way you're pounding that knee?"

He let out a groan of frustration, grabbing her by

the shoulders. "Even when your own life is a disaster, maybe *because* your own life is a disaster, you spend every waking moment meddling in other people's affairs. Like Eric and whatever the hell it is that made him lose fifteen minutes of beauty sleep! Who cares? He'll sort it out. And if he doesn't, well, that's his problem, isn't it? And now my damn knee." He stopped. His voice dropped, but it was perfectly cold. "Lizzie, here's the bottom line—I don't want anything to do with you until you make your mind up to stop rescuing other people and start saving yourself."

As he wheeled around and started beating a path around the outside of the ballroom, Lizzie stopped chasing him. His retreating back disappeared into the trees, and she shouted, "Oh, yeah? Tell me about it, Mr. Firefighter, with the bum knee from rescuing babies from burning buildings! Who's the dyed-in-the-wool rescuer here? Who carried me off from this very ballroom?"

Joe didn't answer, and Lizzie didn't know what to think.

Upset, powerless, livid, she kicked the toe of her tennis shoe into the verandah foundation. "Ow. Ow."

Now she was upset, powerless and in pain. Just what she needed.

She limped back into the hotel, not exactly sure what to do next. Her need to help other people out of their jams was so much a part of her, she didn't think she could just turn it off, the way Joe seemed to want her to. And she thought it was pretty lousy of him to ask, besides!

"I understand about setting limits," she said woefully. "But what could possibly be wrong with trying to help Eric this morning? And why is Fate doing this to me, sending me Joe and then turning him into such a stubborn, clueless maniac?"

While her mind was still spinning, she wandered back through the lobby. She supposed she had nowhere else to go but the Prince Siegfried Suite.

"Ooops." She'd almost run over Anne Crumm, Genevieve's much beleaguered secretary, who seemed as harried and edgy as always. Maybe even a little more so. Anne seemed nice enough, and she certainly had her hands full with Genevieve. Seeing Anne's agitation, Lizzie was very tempted. Oh, what the heck? There was nobody left to be mad at her now. "Anne, I don't mean to pry, but is there anything I can help with?"

"Yes." Anne's slender shoulders were set with determination. "I'm going to the wedding tonight, and well, I'm really sick of plain suits and button-down blouses. I heard Petsy Thorpe talking about all the clothes you gave her, from your catalog. They sound really different and..." she hesitated "...they sound beautiful. I don't suppose you'd have anything to fit me?"

"Wow." Lizzie examined Anne with new eyes. A makeover? Getting to play fairy godmother for a sweet, retiring young woman who wanted to be Cinderella for one night? "You bet. I would love to!"

As she shepherded Anne up to the suite, her head was still spinning, but this time she was consumed with wardrobe ideas to suit Anne's shy beauty. This was going to be such fun!

"And we'll show Joe Bellamy who is and isn't allowed to lend a helping hand," she muttered.

"What did you say?"

"Um, nothing." She smiled. "You know, Anne, I have all kinds of things that are going to look *so* great on you...."

Chapter Twelve

Genevieve's assistant had long since departed, and wonder of wonders, the Prince Siegfried Suite was dead calm.

Clean, neat, with everything aired out and livable, the place seemed strange and foreign. Of course, it had seemed strange and foreign with Zurik and Storm hanging from the wallpaper, too. Now every trace of Lizzie's two fiancés was missing, except for a lingering odor of varnish in the master bedroom, and the half-finished painting propped against the bed.

"It was a lousy portrait anyway," Lizzie said loudly, her words echoing in the empty suite. Okay, so Eric looked good, gazing down from the canvas. "Aaa-chooo." She backed into the parlor and closed the door firmly. "I suppose I could try to convince Caroline that it's meant to be pop art, but the fact that her head is missing from the painting might annoy her."

She didn't know whether to be more surprised by the fact that the suite had been restored to elegance so easily, or that those unruly louts, Zurik and Storm, had left so meekly.

Not Saffron. Saffron hadn't checked out—her bags were still heaped in the double bedroom, and her cosmetics and paraphernalia were in the bath. But she hadn't shown her tiny, heart-shaped face or her tousled auburn curls all afternoon.

As Lizzie hoisted herself into the horrifying ugly, wider than the Mississippi, pink-embroidered-on-pink-bridesmaid dress, she missed Saffron. Her friend's sinfully funny jibes about the dress would've helped ease the pain.

"Oh, brother," she said, taking a spin in front of the mirror, "this getup is *so* not me."

She didn't know which was worse, the yards of puffy fabric, embroidered with darker pink swans on a pale-pink background, the poochy butt bow that resembled a throw pillow, or the extravagant, impossibly wide, flying saucer of a hat, dripping with chiffon.

At least she could hide her face under the hat.

Yep, she definitely missed Saffron. But she missed Joe, too.

She never had gotten to tell him about how magnificent she'd been, dismissing the extra fiancés with a wave of her hand. She'd never had the chance to ask him what the heck happened at the bachelor party that ended up with men jumping—or being thrown?—overboard. Or if he knew whether Bianca's baby belonged to Eric. Or who Eric had fallen in love with that made him so desperately unhappy.

"I never even got the details on how he hurt his

knee," she whispered. His hero story. She imagined it so vividly, with Joe all smoky and wet, searching for the one small child, or pregnant woman, or even a kitty, left behind in a smoldering building. He'd have called out to them, so intent on his search that he didn't see the burning timber falling from the sky until it was too late, and his leg was trapped....

That didn't fit the injury as she'd been able to see it, or the scars on his knee, but she liked the story.

Whatever happened, he was brave and bold, she was sure of that.

Brave and bold...unlike her, the Weenie of the Western World, too scared to face up to her mistakes and be done with it. She had been telling herself—and even Joe—that this was all Saffron's fault, that Lizzie had just been swept up by circumstances beyond her control. But it wasn't true, was it?

Mostly she just didn't want to look stupid in front of the people at this wedding. Oh, yeah, she was bold and brave all right.

And it went back further than that. Even back in the earliest days of The Velvet Fig, she'd known Saff well enough to be sure disaster would happen when Saff went out looking for capital. She'd closed her eyes and hoped for the best, knowing full well it was a really stupid way to do business.

Ultimately, it was Lizzie's company, and her responsibility to put things right, to take her lumps, to reforge The Velvet Fig.

"Which," she said suddenly, "I am going to do."

She grabbed her floppy bridesmaid hat and jammed her hands into the short pink gloves that matched the dress. "Bouquet?" she asked aloud. "Oh, it must be downstairs."

After abandoning the elevator because her skirts wouldn't fit, she was forced to carry her skirts à la Scarlett O'Hara to make it down the curving mahogany staircase. She found, to her surprise, that the hotel lobby was quite deserted. Where was everyone?

Lizzie hurried out to the billowing pink-and-white striped tent off to the side of the Folly, where the bridal party was lined up and waiting. Facing the Folly, guests were already seated on white-fabric-draped chairs, and that same poor harpist from last night was back to Bach, sending gentle, pretty melodies rippling over the crowd.

An altar had been created right there, under the protective wall of the crumbling faux castle, and there were pink and white roses everywhere. As Lizzie took stock of the setting, she saw a veritable tidal wave of flowers. The fragrance was overpowering.

Behind the ruins of the Folly, which was as fake as Lizzie's fiancés, the clear blue water of the pond reflected a cloudless summer sky. A pair of swans glided through the water, arching their necks into the ubiquitous heart shape that decorated Swan's Folly up one side and down the other. If you didn't know better, you might think those swans were swimming on cue, just to create the perfect picture for the wedding of the millennium.

Genevieve Knox wouldn't have it any other way.

Wow. It was so romantic. A little overblown for

Lizzie's taste, but if you were going to have a huge society wedding, this certainly fit the bill.

"Elizabeth, where have you been?" Genevieve hissed. She looked fit to be tied, drained, on the edge of hysteria. "You're late!"

Lizzie blinked. She thought she was on time. Had they set up the schedule without telling her? "I thought the wedding was at six. I'm fifteen minutes early, aren't I?"

"Fifteen minutes? As a bridesmaid, you were expected to be here two hours ago, to assist Caroline, to pose for charming candid photos of the bridesmaids with their heads together, laughing at the..." Mrs. Knox's voice faded away. "Oh, never mind. Just get into line behind Bianca, will you? Winnifred, there is a smudge on your shoe. Disgraceful. Anne? Anne? Where are Elizabeth's flowers?"

As obediently as she could manage, Lizzie stood where she was told, clutching the lavish light-and-dark-pink rose bouquet somebody shoved her way. She'd never seen a bouquet shaped like a beehive. Like Caroline's hair, as a matter of fact.

Oh, dear. Caroline's wedding gown, the one with each minuscule bead and stitch hand-sewn by a fleet of blind Belgian nuns, was dreadful. Not as bad as the bridesmaids, but right up there.

The heavy, vanilla-colored brocade, littered with hundreds of tiny, beaded swans, looked stiff and harsh, not unlike her hairdo. She resembled the world's largest Dolly Vardes cake. Caroline's perfect pearls were in place, and her face was rigid as she stared blankly ahead of her.

Without moving a muscle, she ordered her mother, "Let's get this show on the road."

"Are we ready?" Genevieve asked, her eyelid twitching as she went over each and every person with a fine-tooth comb.

But Lizzie wasn't paying attention. There was a slit in the pink-and-white tent curtain, and if she tipped her head and peered up under her silly hat, she could catch a glimpse of the groomsmen, filing in on their side of the altar.

Her heart turned over. Joe.

They were all there—as she watched, Viv and Budge slipped into their rows behind Eric; Neill, Kevin, Joe stood tall; even Nana vamped until ready, on the verge of prancing to her seat.

"All right," Genevieve whispered loudly. Anne, resplendent in an Edwardian-looking suit straight from Lizzie's catalog, trailed her boss, checking things off on a clipboard. "When I give the cue, they'll seat Nana—"

But Lizzie jumped out of line. "Excuse me," she told Genevieve. "I'm really sorry. There's something I have to do."

Genevieve gasped and tried to grab her by the butt bow, but Lizzie was too quick for the older woman. She charged up the center aisle, stopping squarely in the middle, between the immaculate rows of guests. Then she inhaled sharply, nearly choked on the scent of fifteen thousand roses, coughed slightly, and raised her chin.

There was a pause, as the assembly held its collective breath.

"I'm really sorry to bother you all at a time like

this. I know you have better things to do," she began. "But there's something I just wanted you all to know."

Back at the beginning of the aisle, Nana Lambert shouted, "What? What did she say?"

Nothing was going to stop Lizzie now. She declared loudly, "There have been some misunderstandings here this week. So, to clarify things, I need to tell you that I am not and never have been engaged. To anyone."

Budge bellowed, "What kind of game is this?" and leapt from his seat, but Viv turned around and said, "Sit down, Budge. This is getting good. Go ahead, Liz, hon." She waved a hand gaily. "You just keep right on."

"Like I said, I'm not engaged. Storm Schrempf, the man that some of you know as my fiancé, is really just Saffron's brother. He is not and never has been my boyfriend or my fiancé or my lover."

"Storm? You and Storm?" Viv howled. Now it was her turn to bound to her feet, and Budge's turn to tell her to be quiet and sit down.

Lizzie felt a zone of tranquillity, like the eye of a hurricane, surround her. Was that her voice she heard, gabbing on and on?

"As for the other one, Zurik—well, he was supposed to paint my wedding present to Caroline and Eric. I'm sorry to let that cat out of the bag, but he didn't finish, so I don't have a present for the happy couple, but I'll get something to them, I promise. Not that that's important," she added. "But Zurik isn't my boyfriend, my lover or my fiancé, either. Everyone clear now? Elizabeth Rose Muldoon has no fiancé, no husband, no boyfriend, no nothing. After the wedding, I'll be happy to answer your questions and see if we can't explain this to everyone's satisfaction."

She faltered. "I just... I just wanted to make that one point clear." Sweeping around with a rustle of sickly pink tulle, she sent Joe a level, longing stare. "So, for the record, I am very much alone. That's all I had to say. Thank you for listening. Uh, carry on."

As she lifted her skirts and hiked back to the bridal party tent, she heard Viv and Budge start an argument with each other, Genevieve let out several piercing shrieks, and Nana demand to know what had been said.

People tittered, and there was some nervous chatter, but mostly things calmed down. Lizzie felt as if a huge weight had been lifted from her shoulders.

But as she got back to the pink-and-white tent, Genevieve snatched at her gloved hand. "You," she snarled, "are in big trouble, missy. My money is out of your shoddy little company, now and forever. Now get your butt bow up there and stand like a lady, do you hear me?"

"Yes, ma'am." She didn't dare add anything else.

As the music picked up again, playing their cues, Lizzie was mashed into her proper place in the order.

But then there was a rustle at the altar, and Lizzie hazarded a glance that way, expecting to see a proper clergyman slip behind the podium. But if that was Reverend Lovejoy, Lizzie was the pope.

Saffron? Lizzie's jaw dropped. It was definitely Saffron, emerging from behind the podium, stretching to her full five feet nothing.

What in the world was she doing up there, especially wearing a sunshine-yellow velvet tank dress that clearly clashed with the rest of the dress code and a hat big enough to look just right on the *Titanic*? In fact, it was big enough to *sink* the *Titanic*.

Saffron, playing a part in the wedding?

"Psst, Lizzie," Bianca whispered, looking unbearably curious. "What church is Saffron ordained in?"

Almost ready to be guided to her own seat, Genevieve said, "Shhh" rather loudly.

"Church?" Lizzie tried not to smile. "Saffron isn't ordained in any church. She's a member of..." She tried to remember the name of the place. "The Cloister of the Goddess of Universal Bliss and Sunshine. Or something like that. They're into spreading joy. That's why they love weddings." Lizzie shrugged. Nothing Saffron did ever surprised her, but where was the regular minister? "I think all the members of the Cloister of the Goddess perform ceremonies, actually. You know, they get those mail order certificates, to make it legal."

Prepared to shush them again, Genevieve instead turned very pale as she processed Lizzie's words. "Cloister of the what?" she echoed. "Did you say..." Her voice grew fainter. "Did you say *goddess? Good lord."

But Genevieve was swept away to be seated, with no time to do more than gulp, glance at Saffron and her mustard-colored dress, give out a little moan and gulp again.

Things happened quickly after that. Genevieve sank into her seat next to Hainsworth, ribbons were unfurled down the aisle, and then it was Lizzie's turn.

She tried to keep to the music, dipping slightly, focusing straight ahead. On her right, Budge leaned into the aisle, his brows beetled, his cheeks puffed out. "I need to talk to you as soon as this shindig is over."

Well, gee, what a surprise.

One step more, and Viv got her say. "You go, girl! Don't worry about ol' Budge—I'll talk him into leaving his investment alone, and I'll make up whatever Gen pulls out."

Lizzie smiled, dizzily finding her spot at the end of the line. She kept her eyes on her bouquet, not daring to peek out from under her hat to see what Joe was doing over there. Had he forgiven her? Had her public display of contrition impressed him or humiliated him further?

Now she had to wait until the entire ceremony stuttered to a close to find out.

The other bridesmaids joined her in their turn, and then nasty little ring-bearer Lambie and squeaky flower girl Fawn, who seemed determined to launch her rose petals rather than merely drop them, and to provide a running commentary on where and how she'd hurled them. She and Lambie plunked themselves down on the grass, happy to be off their feet, and they started hitting each other.

"Dear God," Genevieve whimpered.

Given who was officiating, a prayer to "dear goddess" might have been more appropriate.

"Finally," Lizzie muttered under her breath, as the harpist trilled her fingers over the processional, and Caroline took center stage. The audience rose to watch the bride stagger down the aisle, her whole body held so tightly you could've bounced dimes off her chin.

Even her veil was stiff and unyielding. Lizzie managed a smile for Caroline. Every bride was beautiful, wasn't she? And Caro would've been, if only she could learn to lighten up.

Why *was* the bride so unhappy? Not to mention the groom?

Lizzie had never been present at a car wreck, but she was beginning to feel as if she were up close and personal with the functional equivalent.

Instead of "Dearly beloved," Saffron opened with, "Welcome, cherished spirits of light and goodness!"

She droned on, something about moving toward the sweet nectar of bliss and joy and finding the goddess in all of them, but the tension rose, palpable and dense, as they all stood dutifully before the Folly. No one moved. The seconds ticked away.

Was this taking forever, or was it her imagination? What was Joe doing over there? Should he really have been standing still on his battered knee all this time?

Lizzie's gaze skittered out from under the shade of her immense hat, inching down the line of bridesmaids, past the bride, over the groom and the best man, skipping past the groomsmen in their formal cutaway coats.

She found him at the end of the line. *Joe.*

Well aware no one could see her face, Lizzie had the luxury of grinning at him like a love-struck fool. No matter what else happened with this bizarre waxworks wedding, Joe stood head and shoulders above the others, a real man amid a sea of impostors.

Stalwart as he was, he was not paying attention to the ceremony. As Lizzie watched, Joe twisted, peering up at the sky. Her wide-screen picture hat made following his gaze impossible, but she could hear the whir of helicopter blades high above.

"Paparazzi," someone whispered in a nearby row.

People began to rustle and cough behind their hands, but Saffron wasn't finished with her soliloquy on the purity of the marriage covenant and how it connected mere mortals to the eternal earth and the infinite stars.

"Only through this mystical union, this mingling of souls, may we dissolve the differences between male and female, yin and yang, man and woman, Adam and Eve, Scylla and Charybdis—"

"Get on with it," Genevieve snarled from the front row.

"Okay, okay." Saffron sighed, but she moved on. With a sulky pout, she asked, "Does anyone here know any reason, yadda, yadda, yadda?"

Genevieve started using words no high-toned lady should ever utter in public. To her credit, her curses weren't very loud, so at least no one more than a few feet away could hear them. Besides, the helicopters were getting louder, dipping closer, their blades chopping up the air and starting to agitate the canvas tents.

"Well?" Saffron prompted, holding on to her colossal hat with one hand. She raised her voice. "Anybody want to jump in?"

There was a definite pause. Saffron looked at Lizzie, waited, looked at Bianca, waited, and finally shrugged.

"Okay, well, I think we're set on that score. Caroline," Saffron began, practically shouting to be heard above those awful helicopters, "do you take this man, Eric, as your lawful wedded soul mate, to nurture and support, to cherish and encourage, to give roots *and* give wings, in harmony and in unity, so long as your souls shall inhabit this mortal plane?"

Except for the buzz of chopper blades, silence hung heavy in the makeshift chapel in front of the Folly.

"Caroline?" Saffron yelled. She looked up into the sky at the invading force, screwed up her face, and tried again. "Do you take Eric?"

No response.

No one said a word. Finally, Genevieve hissed, "Say it, Caroline."

So she did. Caroline shouted, *"No!"* which was not exactly the word anyone expected to hear. It seemed to echo and bounce off the soft gray stone of the Folly wall.

Lizzie gripped her bouquet so hard a rose popped off and smacked her in the chest. Nana Lambert's voice rose above the circling 'copters. "Did she say no?"

Her voice quavering, Caroline cried, "I refuse to marry him because he slept with *her* last night!" And she pointed a shaky finger in the direction of Lizzie's half of the congregation.

Nana demanded, "What did she say?"

Now everyone was staring at Lizzie, who choked, "Me? He didn't sleep with me! I was with…"

She tipped back her head so she could get a good look at Joe, to try to gauge whether he wanted to acknowledge last night's tryst at Thistle Cottage. Given her history at this event, she wasn't sure anyone would believe her anyway.

But Joe remained impassive, difficult to read. Lizzie stood her ground. Proudly, she announced, "I was with Joe. Right there—bachelor number three. Joe Bellamy. All night."

Viv Bellamy hooted with laughter. "This is too much!"

"It's true." Joe's expression was guarded, but he nodded. She hoped she detected a note of humor in his voice when he said, "What with two fiancés *and* me, I don't think Lizzie had time to fool around with Eric, too."

Someone must have believed him, because the collective gazes switched to Bianca.

"Don't look at me," she said quickly.

Caroline's shoulders sagged as much as they could inside her armor-plated gown. Angrily, she shouted, "I didn't mean either of you. I meant *her!* See? Eric's not even bothering to deny it."

Once again, heads turned. This was starting to look like a tennis match.

Well, Eric did seem a little flushed. People in the back stood up, and the nearer rows craned their necks. It was clear they were all looking for the Scarlet Woman of the moment, whoever it was who'd supposedly slept with Eric last night.

But who was it? Who was Caroline talking about?

By now, the helicopters were so close that even Caroline's weighty veil whipped up, and one of the tents began to gallop like a runaway stallion. Caroline shook a finger in Eric's face, wailing, weeping, and he responded, but Lizzie couldn't hear a word they were saying.

People pointed and jostled and the hum of gossip grew to a roar. Her feet were tapping with nervous energy, and she had to use both hands to keep her chiffon-draped hat on her head. Lizzie was bursting with a need to help out, but what could she do? She couldn't think of anything. Surely there was something *someone* could do—

But Caroline ended the suspense, wheeling unsteadily in her massive dress, stomping back down the aisle, heaving her bouquet in the general direction of her mother.

Lizzie hadn't even had time to react to that astounding development when suddenly, out of the blue, she heard a huge rush of sound from above. One minute she was standing there, minding her own business, and the next, something very hard and very heavy, wrapped in yards of surging white silk, bonked her on the head, crashed painfully into her back and knocked her flat.

What in the name of...? She was trapped. She couldn't breathe, couldn't move. Choking whiteness. She saw stars everywhere in her periphery, stars on an infinite field of white. White everywhere, flapping. Was she inside a cloud? Heaven?

Just as she was about to really panic, the veil of white was lifted. Like magic. She saw roses now, the Folly, the sky. And Joe's handsome face silhouetted against them.

His face descended right over hers, warm and alive, and she began to think maybe she wasn't dead after all. His mouth covered hers, and she felt a rush of hungry desire. No, definitely not dead.

"Lizzie, stop kissing me. I'm doing mouth-to-mouth."

She tried to ask him what had happened, but nothing came out except a choked whistle. There was noise and confusion everywhere, people shouting and shoving, as Joe bent over her.

"Are you all right?" he asked anxiously. "Lizzie, can you hear me? If you can kiss back, you can hear me, right?"

She nodded, but she couldn't get words out yet. "Anything...happen...Bellamy wedding," she joked.

But Joe's face was white and strained as he carefully, swiftly, gathered her up into his arms, shoving aside yards of pink-on-pink tulle. No Fireman's Carry this time—he cradled her against his chest, pushing through the melee, transporting her away from the Folly with all due haste.

"Can't...leave," she breathed, trying to see around him. Did Caroline flee? Where was Eric?

What happened to the wedding? What happened to *her?*

Joe answered none of her questions, sweeping her away from there, rushing up the lawn and into the hotel. He paused, reaching under her to hit the button for the aged brass elevator, clasping her close to him.

"I'm taking you to your room," he whispered, pressing his lips to her forehead. "You stay quiet, okay? You need to lie down, get this dress undone, splash some cool water on your face."

Undoing her dress and getting into bed with Joe sounded like an excellent idea. Who cared what happened at the wedding? She had better things to do.

Joe maneuvered them into the cage, swinging her legs clear as he shoved the door closed, and then braced them both for the inevitable rocky lift. But as the elevator passed between the first and second floors, it gave out a thump, a squeal and a long, rusty screech. And then it went nowhere.

"Uh-oh." They weren't moving—she had been up and down in this elevator enough times to know what it felt like as it lurched along. And this wasn't it. "Joe, are we stuck?"

"Lizzie, you're talking again!" He rained kisses on her face with relief.

The kisses were lovely. Lizzie was close to just giving in and enjoying it. But not like this. "I think you'd better put me down," she said weakly. "I'm feeling a lot better. Honest."

But his arms stayed banded firmly around her.

"Joe, put me down!" she insisted. "We don't know how long we'll be stuck in here, and you should never have hauled me around like that in the first place with your knee.''

"You worry far too much about my knee.''

"Somebody has to, since you don't!'' She pushed at his chest until he finally relented, setting her gently on her feet. "That's better. Phew.''

She was still a little dizzy, and the air in the elevator was close and stuffy. As he released her, she stumbled, righting herself against Joe.

"You may have a concussion, you know,'' he persisted, running his hands cautiously over her head, checking her over in the dim light.

"I don't have a concussion. I just had the wind knocked out of me.'' But she kept a hand on Joe to steady herself. "What happened, anyway? I saw Caroline throw her bouquet into the second row, and the next thing I knew, I was flat as a pancake with some huge white thing all over me.'' Her eyes widened. "Did a tent blow on top of me?''

"No, a parachutist jumped on top of you.''

She knocked him in the chest. "Get out.''

"I'm totally serious.''

"A parachute? But what...? A reporter, you think?'' She wrinkled her forehead, trying to piece together the hazy memories. "I think I heard somebody say there were paparazzi.''

"Yeah, it's probably the best guess.'' He frowned at her. "I'd feel better if you sat down.''

Almost without thinking, Lizzie slid down the wall, landing in a pool of pink tulle. "Ooops.''

Joe was at her side in an instant. "I was right. You're not okay.''

"Just a little woozy, that's all.''

"Here. Lean forward. Let me…" His clever fingers found the row of small hooks and eyes, unfastening them one by one, until the fabric gapped from the neckline to the mammoth bow, just below her waist.

"Better," she murmured. She still felt lightheaded, but cooler now, and tingly where his fingers had brushed her skin. She scooted out from the wall. "How about the rest of it?"

"Lizzie…"

She tried to put on an innocent face. "I think I'd be more comfortable, that's all."

His expression was dubious, but he undid the hooks all the way down. Lizzie shook out of it, rubbing her bare shoulders, feeling much better in her camisole and petticoat.

Joe averted his eyes. "I, uh, better take a look around—see if there's a call box or an alarm or something."

He poked into every corner of that elevator, but couldn't find anything remotely useful. Swearing to himself, he charted the same path over again, methodically checking every nook and cranny. "There has to be something."

"Joe, why don't you relax?" Almost back to her old self, Lizzie sat in the corner and watched his progress. "Even if you found an alarm, no one would hear it. They're all at the wedding. Or what's left of the wedding." She patted the floor next to her. "Come sit by me."

His eyes were hooded. "I know what happened the last time you said that."

"Like you didn't enjoy it."

"I never said that."

Lizzie half reclined on the floor of the elevator, propping her head in one hand. "So what's the problem? I did what you wanted—I made my big announcement. And I also tried to repair my, ahem, doormat ways."

That got his interest. He edged closer. "Oh, yeah?"

"Yeah." A mischievous smile lit her face. "Wait till you hear. I threw Zurik and Storm out on their keisters."

"No?"

"Oh, yes." By the time she finished the story—with a bit of creative embroidery—they were both laughing. He was alongside her on the floor, his long legs stretched out next to hers, his arm around her so that she could lean into his shoulder. It was very nice. "And by the time I got back, the whole place was clean as a whistle. You'd never know they were there."

"I saw Saffron at the wedding breakfast, but she kind of sniffed and went the other direction." Joe shrugged. "I thought it was because I punched Zurik at Viv's place." His lips curved into a crooked smile. "It's more likely she thinks I'm a bad influence on you."

Lizzie sobered, meeting his gaze, ready to probe deeper. "And what do you think?"

A pause hung between them. "I think that you got sucked into something really stupid that you had a hard time getting out of. And I think..." He took her hands into his own. "I think we're both addicted to rescue missions, but maybe I'm a little better at setting boundaries than you are. But maybe you're a little better at trusting people than I am."

She couldn't believe she was hearing this from Joe. "I think I might be able to set better boundaries," she admitted. "After all, it doesn't do anybody any good if I'm getting walked on."

"Absolutely," Joe replied with a smile. He tipped his head in and kissed her, slow and sweet, a promise for the future. "And I can help you. If you help me."

Wow. For the first time, Lizzie thought his help might be a very good idea.

"Do you hear that?" Lizzie pricked up her ears. "It's music. I think it's coming from the ballroom downstairs."

Joe scrambled to his feet. "Think there's any chance they'd hear us if we jump up and down and scream?"

"Nope. Not with an orchestra playing." Lizzie sighed and relaxed against the wall. "I guess the wedding and the reception went on after all. Oh well. I'm not sure it matters." She smiled mistily up at Joe. "Here, with just the two of us, things are so much nicer. It's like the world belongs to us, don't you think?"

Joe inclined his head. "Sounds like that song you liked." He extended a hand. "Want to dance?"

"Joe," she laughed, "that was 'Embraceable You.' Gershwin! This sounds like disco. Totally different head."

"I don't care. Do you?"

"Normally, I would care. But under the circumstances..." Lizzie rose as gracefully as she could manage, taking his hand, spinning into his arms. She rested her head on his shoulder, leaned in, drifting happily to the music. "Mmmm. This is nice."

"Mmm-hmmm."

They danced for some time, as song melted into song, as body melted into body. It was almost an afterthought when his lips brushed hers and her arms tightened, when his caresses became more heated and they sank to the floor together.

With the wide circle of her tulle skirt as a blanket underneath them, they shed their clothing, slow and unhurried. And this time, when they made love, each kiss, each touch, was languorous, tender, achingly sweet. And when she lay curled in his arms, she knew, without a doubt, that she wasn't willing to do without Joe Bellamy for even a minute after this.

"Joe, I have something I have to tell you," she whispered.

He held himself very still. "It better not be that you have another fiancé hiding somewhere."

"Of course not." She snuggled closer. "It's that I think you're my destiny."

"Your destiny, huh?"

"I know that must sound weird to you, but you haven't met my mother," she told him. "When you do, it will make more sense."

"If you say so."

"Joe, the thing is…" The words were forming on her lips when he met her mouth, blocking her confession.

"You were going to say that you love me," he said, drawing away when she was breathless. "I know."

"And you love me, too." It was a statement, not a question.

"See?" he teased. "I do understand the meaning of destiny."

An amazing feeling, of joy and karma and fate—all that mystical union of souls stuff Saffron had been preaching at the wedding—filled Lizzie's heart.

"You know, of course," she told him, a little shy, "now you really ought to marry me."

"I'd love to." He winced, adjusting his bad leg, draping Lizzie across him. "But I refuse to get engaged to you. No one would believe us anyway. So I'll only agree to marry you if we do it tomorrow morning, first thing, no engagement and no preliminaries. What do you say?"

"I say yes." Lizzie laughed out loud, and the happy, crazy sound of it reverberated in their brass cage, their haven at Swan's Folly. "Maybe not tomorrow. But soon. Because after all, I'm fresh out of fiancés."

HARLEQUIN® AMERICAN ROMANCE®

You are cordially invited to

THE WEDDING PARTY

With three of your favorite
American Romance® authors

PLACE:
Swan's Folly
Lake Geneva, Wisconsin

DATE:
#782 July 1999
LIZZIE'S LAST-CHANCE FIANCÉ
Julie Kistler

#786 August 1999
RSVP...BABY
Pamela Browning

#791 September 1999
ASSIGNMENT: GROOM!
Jacqueline Diamond

BRIDE & GROOM: To be announced!

Available wherever Harlequin books are sold.

HARLEQUIN®
Makes any time special ™

Look us up on-line at: http://www.romance.net   HARWP2

Looking For More Romance?

Visit Romance.net

Look us up on-line at: http://www.romance.net

Check in daily for these and other exciting features:

Hot off the press

View all current titles, and purchase them on-line.

What do the stars have in store for you?

Horoscope

Hot deals

Exclusive offers available only at Romance.net

Plus, don't miss our interactive quizzes, contests and bonus gifts.

PWEB

HARLEQUIN
AMERICAN ❖ ROMANCE®

*They're handsome, they're sexy, they're
determined to remain single.
But these two "bachelors" are about to
receive the shock of their lives...*

OOPS! STILL MARRIED!

**August 1999—#787 THE OVERNIGHT GROOM
by Elizabeth Sinclair**
Grant Waverly must persuade Katie Donovan to
continue their newly discovered marriage for just two
more intimate weeks....

**September 1999—#790 OVERNIGHT FATHER
by Debbi Rawlins**
Matthew Monroe never forgot the woman he'd once
married for convenience. And now Lexy Monroe
needs the man from whom she's kept
one little secret....

Look for the special *Oops! Still Married!*
duet, coming to you soon—only from
Harlequin American Romance®!

The honeymoon is just beginning...

Available at your favorite retail outlet.

HARLEQUIN®
Makes any time special ™

Look us up on-line at: http://www.romance.net   HAROOPS

COMING NEXT MONTH

#785 THE LAST STUBBORN COWBOY by Judy Christenberry
4 Tots for 4 Texans
With his friends married and in a family way, Mac Gibbons thought the
bet was over, and he was safe from the matchmaking moms of Cactus,
Texas. That is, until he stopped to help a lady in distress and looked
down into the blue eyes of new doc Samantha Collins...and her baby
daughter. A daughter who looked amazingly just like Mac!

#786 RSVP...BABY by Pamela Browning
The Wedding Party
The last thing Bianca D'Alessandro needed was to be a bridesmaid at a
family wedding. Especially since she'd be bringing a pint-size guest no
one knew about. She could pass off the whispers, but she couldn't avoid
the best man, Neill Bellamy—the father of her secret baby....

#787 THE OVERNIGHT GROOM by Elizabeth Sinclair
Oops! Still Married!
Grant Waverly's career was his mistress...until he found out he
was married! Kathleen Donovan had been his one true love—and
apparently his wife for the past seven years, though neither one knew
it. But now that Grant had a wife, he intended to keep her!

#788 DEPUTY DADDY by Charlotte Maclay
Lawman Johnny Fuentes didn't know what to do with the beautiful
but very pregnant woman with amnesia who was found wandering in
town—except take her home. Trouble was, soon she began believing he
was her husband!

Look us up on-line at: http://www.romance.net

HARLEQUIN CELEBRATES

In August 1999, Harlequin American Romance® delivers a month of our best authors, best miniseries and best romances as we celebrate Harlequin's 50th Anniversary!

Look for these other terrific American Romance® titles at your favorite retail stores:

THE LAST STUBBORN COWBOY (#785)
by Judy Christenberry

RSVP...BABY (#786)
by Pamela Browning

THE OVERNIGHT GROOM (#787)
by Elizabeth Sinclair

DEPUTY DADDY (#788)
by Charlotte Maclay

HARLEQUIN®
Makes any time special ™

Look us up on-line at: http://www.romance.net   H50HAR/L